Joseph Parrish Thompson

Bryant Gray : The student, the Christian, the soldier

Joseph Parrish Thompson

Bryant Gray : The student, the Christian, the soldier

ISBN/EAN: 9783337131678

Printed in Europe, USA, Canada, Australia, Japan

Cover: Foto ©Raphael Reischuk / pixelio.de

More available books at **www.hansebooks.com**

Your affectionate Son
G. C. Bryant Gra,

BRYANT GRAY:

THE STUDENT, THE CHRISTIAN, THE SOLDIER.

BY

JOSEPH P. THOMPSON, D. D.,

PASTOR OF THE BROADWAY TABERNACLE CHURCH

NEW YORK:

ANSON D. F. RANDOLPH,

No. 770 BROADWAY, COR. NINTH ST.

1864.

TO

William Cullen Bryant,

THE LIFE-LONG ADVOCATE OF THE RIGHTS OF MAN,

This Memorial

OF ONE WHO BORE HIS NAME TO THE FIELD
IN DEFENSE OF THOSE RIGHTS,

IS RESPECTFULLY

INSCRIBED.

I.

The Campaign of 1860.

"YOU will vote for 'Honest Abe,' of course;" I said, to a young friend who stood directly in front of me in the poll-line, on the eventful 6th of November, 1860.

He had come to cast his maiden-vote, and as he was a frequent attendant upon my ministry, I felt a paternal interest in the opening of his citizen-life.

"What! Not vote for Mr. Lincoln!" I exclaimed, as half-blushing, half-laughing, he shook his head in the negative; "what *can* you mean? No man must go amiss or hang back, to-day."

"I start for Texas, to-morrow," he an-

swered, " for health and business ; and if I
am ever to come back alive, I had better be
able to say that I did n't vote for Mr. Lincoln ; so I shall go the State Republican
ticket, and not vote for President at all."

Was he then a coward ? I must confess
that, at the moment, I pitied him for lack
of decision ; little thinking what elements
of courage and patriotism lay dormant in
his mild, blue eyes, and what manly daring
would yet be exhibited by this lithe, delicate boy, in fighting down the treason
against which he hesitated to cast a ballot.

This little incident gives the condensed
history of an epoch that now seems a by-
gone century ; when, in thirteen States of
the Union, a social terrorism, as arbitrary as
the " Bomba " rule in Naples, compelled men
to speak with 'bated breath of human rights
and liberty, and made torture or the gibbet
the penalty of an opinion or a vote looking
toward the deliverance of the enslaved.
Should slavery as an organic system survive
the war, not all the blood of our brave

defenders can wipe out that hideous des-
potism from the land ; for slavery creates
and demands such terrorism as its own
defense. We must obliterate slavery, or
we lose the whole cost and pains of the
war. We must fight until the country is
made free, in every part of it, to each and
every citizen. We must fight until in Richmond, in Charleston, in Montgomery, one
can say, " I voted for Abraham Lincoln in
1860," as unconcernedly as he can speak of
the weather-table in an old almanac.

My young friend soon learned that his
enforced abstinence from voting would not
save his credit with men who were bent
upon the destruction of their country. Before winter was over, he found that he could
remain in Texas only upon condition of
forswearing the Union, and of taking up
arms against it. Then, all his manhood
showed itself. The instant secession was
determined upon by the Convention of the
State, he set his face northward, with a spirit
that his journal clearly shows.

"*April* 4, 1861. — I took my last view of San Antonio, sad, but yet happy that I am leaving such insecurity, lawlessness, and secession rabbles behind me."

At Mobile, on the 12th of April, he received the intelligence of the attack on Fort Sumter. "At this news Mobile was thrown into great excitement ; the majority of the people seemed glad, but many were sad. As for me, I too clearly foresaw the civil war which was to follow. As the wires conveyed the news to every part of the country, the sleeping North rose up against the perfidious South ; the first ball from Fort Moultrie was the signal for the clash of arms. Alas for my country ! *God help Freedom !*"

On reaching Washington, after many perils, he writes (April 18th) : "All through the night I heard the clatter of cavalry in the streets, the note of preparation for the contest. Rouse my countrymen ! To arms ! God be with us !"

The baptism of Freedom was upon him.

He had escaped out of Egypt. He who five months before had hesitated to cast a vote against the threats of the South, was now eager to confront her armies with the sword. Conscience, patriotism, and religion made BRYANT GRAY a hero.

II.

The Worth of a Good Name.

HE bore an honored name. His father, gifted with tastes above his early opportunities for their improvement, had redeemed from the drudgery of apprenticeship in a village store many an hour for communion with Nature, and with poets who were her best interpreters. The poems of Bryant had especially fascinated him, not only by their fidelity to Nature, but by that inward purity and sincerity of soul which they unconsciously unveil. The young shopkeeper made this then new volume of poetry the companion of his walks in the woods and fields of his native Dutchess; committed every line of it to memory; and in the fervor of his admiration, vowed that should he ever have a son, he would name him Bryant, and would train him for a culture that he himself had been denied. Years after, when a clerk in New York, his first-born came as the redemption of this pledge, and WILLIAM CULLEN BRYANT GRAY linked the name of the first American poet to a surname already honored in English literature. It would almost seem that by some subtle poetic affinity without natural kin, the name of Gray had conveyed to this child the pensive and reflective temperament of the author of the Elegy, and that his epitaph was anticipated a century ago—

" A youth to fortune and to fame unknown;
    Fair Science frowned not on his humble birth,
And Melancholy marked him for her own."

The announcement of his baptismal name to Mr. Bryant, brought the following response to his father :

"NEW YORK, May 15, 1841.

"SIR—I should have answered your letter before this, but I put it off from day to day, until I could go to my publishers for a copy of my poems, which I send you, and which you will oblige me by keeping for your son until he is able to read it. I cannot be insensible to the compliment you have paid me in giving him my name, inasmuch as it shows the sincerity of the favorable opinion you are pleased to express of me. I must enjoin upon you, however, to direct his attention to better models of conduct than his namesake. Meantime, present my compliments to the little gentleman, who I hope, will do more honor to the name of Bryant than I have ever done.

"I am, sir, respectfully yours,

"WM. C. BRYANT."

Such a gift from such a source would become a talisman to the imagination of any child as soon as he should be capable of understanding its significance ; but to a boy,

whose nervous organization proved as delicate and sensitive as a girl's ; who, from his
earliest consciousness, seemed to shrink
within himself, shunning the common sports
of boyhood, making few companions on the
street, but courting the society of books,
this volume of poems, imprinted with his
own Christian name, was the magic key that
unlocked to his soul all the wealth of Nature, and that opened within himself the
deeper mysteries of life. His father lost
no opportunity of fostering the associations
of Bryant's christening gift, and the love
of the beautiful and beneficent in Nature
which it was fitted to inspire. In his own
relaxation from city toils, he would spend
the long summer days in the woods and by
the streams, making this child the companion of his rambles, reading to him such
poems as he could comprehend, and teach-
ing him to know and love all that was beautiful in earth, air, and sky.

When the boy was about five years old,
his father read to him, on a soft summer day

in the woods, Bryant's " Lines on Revisiting
the Country," in which the poet describes
the effect of natural scenery upon his own
child in " her fourth bright year :"

" For I have taught her, with delighted eye,
    To gaze upon the mountains—to behold,
With deep affection, the pure, ample sky,
    And clouds along its blue abysses rolled ;
To love the song of waters, and to hear
The melody of winds with charmèd ear."

The boy listened " with delighted eye "
to every word, assenting, by nods and by
audible signs, to each line as it was ex-
plained to him, until the last two were re-
cited ; then he shook his head alternately,
" Yes " and " No." " The Song of Waters,"
said he, " that's just so. I love to hear it,
too ; but the other part is n't right. The
wind does n't make melody ; the wind is
sad." The pensive element in his soul responded to the sighing and wailing of the
wind among the trees. Yet, at that early
age, he would kindle with enthusiasm at the

sight of beauty. At six, his father took
him to the highest peak of the Catskill, and
when the marvellous glory of valley and
river and mountain lay spread before his
view, asked him what he thought of the
prospect. Bryant stood awhile wrapped in
meditation, then slowly answered, " It looks
to me like our Saviour's temptation on the
mountain!" So well were the Gray and
the Bryant blended in his pensive, yet ap-
preciative and admiring soul.

III.

The Man in the Boy.

A GOOD religious training gave a true direction to this thoughtful and susceptible child. His father, though not then professing godliness, rightly appreciated a Christian education, and, by precept and example, taught Bryant to practice virtue and to respect religion; his mother, a devout member of a Baptist church, consecrated him to the service of the Saviour. In early childhood he was always deeply moved by the story of the cross, and he would often repeat to the younger children, in subdued and tender tones, what he had learned at Sabbath-school of the love of Jesus and the glory of heaven. He grew up in the habit of reverence and with a love for holy things.

A tender and gentle spirit seemed in harmony with the pale face and the frail form of his childhood ; and perhaps his own delicate constitution made him more quick to sympathize with the weak and suffering. When a little boy, he once sat up all night nursing a " baby-pigeon ;" he would press the tiny thing to his breast, and as it seemed to lose vitality, he would wrap it carefully in cotton and lay it before the fire, in the hope of warming it into life. He never outgrew this sympathetic habit ; but as he grew older it became a law of considerate kindness toward the neglected and the wronged. When a youth of fourteen, in the Free Academy, he came one day to his father with this case for advice :

" There 's a little Irish boy in my class," said he, " who is very poor, and whose dress is very shabby. His mother is a washerwoman. The boys all despise him. When we walk two and two from the recitation-

2*

room to the chapel, nobody will take his arm ; and when we are out at play, nobody will give him a chance. And yet he is a good boy, and the best mathematician in the class. I have been thinking that I ought to take care of him, and to be his friend. What do you think about it, father ?"

His father told him that if he was willing to part with a suit of his own clothes, he might give it to the boy, and that he could do as he pleased about associating with him. Having equipped his *protegé*, Bryant took him under his wing, walked with him arm in arm, took his part on the play-ground, and fostered him like an elder brother. He had good reason afterward to be proud of the youth whom he thus befriended.

But tenderness and gentleness were not the whole of Bryant's character. He could show pluck when the occasion called for it. A lazy classmate, having to declaim an original piece, applied to Bryant, who excelled in writing, for a composition, for

which he gave him a pecuniary considera-
tion.* But as the orator flourished upon
the stage, the class recognized the style of
his piece, and it was whispered all about,
"*He* couldn't write that ; that is Bryant
Gray's."

When this reached the ear of the speaker,
he went to young Gray in a rage, accused
him of having betrayed him, and threatened
to flog him. Bryant was a mere stripling
by the side of his accuser, but looking him
calmly in the eye, he said, "I have not told
any one your secret."

"You lie, you young scoundrel," retorted
the other, making ready to follow his words
with blows.

Bryant drew up to his full height and
said, "I warn you, that if you touch me, you
will do it at your peril ; for I will not stop
till I get through with you. You are nothing

---

* Had Bryant been more mature in judgment and in
Christian principle, neither love nor money could have
made him a party to an imposition upon his teacher.
But school-boys are not apt to be perfect in that direction

but a big coward." At this unexpected show of pluck, the bully slunk away. Bryant had already the germ of the true soldier.

His amiable and manly qualities needed but the refining touch of grace to make him a good soldier of Christ; and in the great revival of 1857 the needful consecration came. Subdued with the sense of his sinfulness, attracted by the sweet influences of the Cross, which, from his childhood, had so touched his heart, he openly avowed the Saviour as his portion, and joined himself to the communion of the saints in the Seventh Avenue Methodist Episcopal Church.

IV.

Travels and Tastes.

IN the opening of 1855, when Bryant was only in his fourteenth year,* his father withdrew him awhile from the Free Academy, and in the hope of recruiting his constitution, took him to San Antonio, Texas, and there left him in the family of a relative. The boy's letters home give us glimpses of his simple, healthful tastes; of his affectionate disposition, and his ardent piety.

"I hope you are improving in music," he writes to a sister, "for when I return, I intend to learn the flute or violin, and accompany you. 'Oh! that will be joyful, to meet

* He was born September 15, 1839.

to part no more.' So you must learn duets, and be prepared for me, for I can learn very quickly to play. You know my enthusiastic love of music, and that I can hardly live without it. Mary V—— was a splendid player; I wish you were here to see her music—songs of all kinds; but she is gone now, and her earthly songs are heard no more; her Maker hears her heavenly songs, which are far more glorious! Please learn to play well, for you know what enjoyment we can have. Do it for my sake, if not for your own benefit. Music is more food to me than bread; and when I hear good, pure melodies, I feel as if lifted above this earth, and my thoughts involuntarily turn to mother, who now sings and hears the most perfect music."*

To his father he gives some sage and earnest, yet, withal, modest counsel, to emanate from a youth of thirteen:

" What is the use of your working, thinking, plodding your way through New York

---

* His mother had recently died.

so much, I cannot see. Are you poor and obliged to work? No. Have you not enough for your future wants? Yes. Why, then, do you do it? It is a false notion that a man must continue to work all his life till death obliges him to quit. I ask you, What is the object of life? Why are we here on earth? To make money? No! but to serve our Creator, and to add one more to the galaxy of stars that surround him. Better, then, instead of *always* making wealth our goal, to retire and pass the decline of life in happiness, and the contemplation of its continuance when we die. Do not think that I am a preacher or sophist; but think of *it;* for what I say is as plain as the nose on your face. I might say more, but this is sufficient, I think, and I fear I may trespass on the obedience I owe to you. But for your children's sake, do not work so hard—they need you yet; and by so doing, there is every prospect of your living twenty years more."

His free out-door life in Texas, favored

his physical improvement, without relaxing his fondness for study.

"I ride early in the morning, then I teach Willie until 12 o'clock ; I then read until 4 or 5, when we again ride until evening. After supper we retire early. I am just as much of a maniac for fresh air now as yourself. I have changed my mode of living entirely. I don't see how I will stand going to school after this. The open prairies are hardly wide enough for me ; my thoughts are more expansive ; I am more restless now than before. After riding and running about at will, as I have done, and am doing, I can hardly submit to being bound down by strict rules and discipline ; but 'where there is a will, there is a way,' and as I have the will to study and be educated, the way will soon be found.

"Uncle J—— reposes entire confidence in me in every thing, almost too much, I am afraid ; but I will try and merit it. He trusts me to drive aunt and Willie out to ride, which is a great trust for me ; as you know, if any accident should happen, I would be to blame, and could never forgive myself. He trusts me to manage the garden, and a great many business affairs at the house and store, and he talks and reasons with me as if I was as old as himself. This is a very good thing for me, as I have a great fault, namely, a lack of confidence in myself; but with his training and instruction it may be mended."

In May, 1855, by invitation of Major Neighbors, Indian agent, young Gray visited the Camanches upon their reservation near Fort Belknap, and was inducted into the wild freedom of nature. Besides its direct influence in invigorating his constitution, this expedition gave him a taste for camp-life, and for "roughing it" in the open air, which, in after years, made him quite at home in the experiences of a Virginia campaign. He used his pen also to advantage, describing Indian life with a sprightliness and ease worthy of Bayard Taylor. Several of his letters, written when he was not yet fourteen, were published in the

New York *Evening Post.* In one of these occurs a graphic description of his journey from San Antonio to the fort :

"As soon as we had gone our day's journey — which we always planned the day before — we selected a place to encamp, on a creek, or near a spring, and under a tree if we could. Then the mules were turned loose and staked ; that is, tied to a bush or stake with a long rope, so that they could eat grass and not get away. A fire was then made of wood, picked up around, and the coffee put on to boil. Bacon was sliced and fried ; and then, if we wanted bread, some meal was mixed up in a pan with a little water and salt, and baked (this is the recipe for the ' Corn Dodger'). This whole process, after stopping, did not occupy more than twenty minutes ; then we pitched into it, and ate it in five.

" Taking our blankets out of the wagon, we laid one down on a buffalo skin, and wrapped the other around us ; then, with our saddles for a pillow, were soon in a sound sleep. The heavens were our canopy, and often have I lain awake, thinking of my far-off home. and friends, and gazing at some bright star, where I fancied I saw my mother, who, although far away, appeared to be near and watching tenderly over me. Then was the time I thought of home, and knew its value.

" My meals, while here, I take in a cabin, where all the hands eat, and such eating you never saw, or will see. The table-cloth is as black as the ground now, and will be put on for a week yet. All we have is fried bacon, beef and coffee, and bread, regularly every meal ; just the same thing one day after another, the whole year round."

He writes from Fort Belknap, July 6, 1855 :

" To-morrow I am going to the Reserve. I always go by a trail made by the Indians, which is the shortest way. A trail is merely a path formed by horses. It is not generally much wider than this sheet, up and down. It does not try to avoid

mountains and rivers, but goes right over
them. This one goes over three mountains
and two creeks. You ought to see the way
it crosses. It does not turn round a big
rock, but goes right over. I have to make
my young pony go over several about as
high as our basement table. The difficulty
consists in its being steep, and the horse
likely to slip. I go up and down bluffs that
you would think only a circus-rider could
mount; and when a river is swollen, we do
not wait for a boat, but plunge in and swim
over safely. I have gone over this trail
during the night, when I could not see any
thing at all. I had to let my pony go himself, scent the track, which I could not see
any more than if I was blind. Once it
rained, and it was very dark; the thunder
gave deafening peals, and the lightning-flash
occasionally revealed me the road. In the
interval, silence reigned, and I was awe-
struck with the grandeur of the scene. My
good horse sped onward, and I reached
my tent just in time to avoid the rain. It

was not stretched well, and there I lay all night, the water trickling down on my face, in my ears, and on my feet ; it rained tremendously. However, the exposure is beneficial, making me robust and healthy. I do not mind now lying out doors in a drenching rain. It does not hurt me at all. I can undergo exposure and do *do* things which I thought impossible before. I can hardly describe them with a pen, but will reserve them to tell on my return, when they will be much more interesting."

This was an excellent, though an unconscious preparation for his subsequent life in the army.

In his eagerness for adventure, Bryant begged the privilege of accompanying the Agent to a General Council at Clear-Fork, to meet Catemse, the chief of the Camanches. Here, after two days' deliberations, both parties united in smoking the pipe of peace. Writing of this visit, Bryant says :

" As we expect to have some difficulty with the Camanches, unless they will settle

3*

and be content, one of the commanders, with
about twenty soldiers, will go up with us.
Major Neighbors was afraid to let me go,
but I persuaded him, assuring him that I
was not afraid. I do not wish to stay here
without any excitement. If they kill me,
that will be the end of my adventures; and
if they capture me, well and good, for I am
in love with their life, they are so happy
and contented—eating when they can, hunt-
ting, and lying down when exhausted. They
are always on horseback, and that, you
know, is my greatest amusement. . . . .
The women work in the fields, hoe, and
so forth; but the men will soon be made to
work, imitating the white man's example.
They will soon raise their own stock and
vegetables, and will then be able to buy
their own luxuries. When this is accomplished, the United States will cease to
supply them, and will consider them as
citizens, if they wish to become such. This
will be a great triumph for civilization to
accomplish over the savage. It is a much

better expedient than war, and will cost less. They seem to like living in this way better than being wild. They consider us wonders; and when we tell them about our railroads, and the like, they say we tell strange stories—lies!

" It is in contemplation to bring on some of their chiefs, and show them the fruits of civilization, arts, and science."

His passion for savage life, however, was not lasting. Indeed, his rough campaigning, and some minor responsibilities that were brought upon him in the Agency, led him to set a higher value upon a liberal education.

" I have now," he writes, " a chance to detect faults in my education, and I am finding and mending every day. They consist principally in having theories and not practice; however, I now have to practice every thing I know, and all my powers of self-government, etc., are called out daily. It is the best place in the world for me here, in that regard; for I have to shift entirely for myself, besides having the control of this Reserve, which is my business for the present. I feel entirely different; not like a boy, but as a man. The Indians here call me Captain, and show me much respect; also, the Americans residing here call me Mr. and Sir; so you see I am rising in the world. My simple mode of living (pork, beef, coffee, and corn bread invariably) is giving me health, and, at the rate I am now improving, six months will entirely renovate my constitution. I am very fleshy, and my cheeks are quite red. Major N. says he never saw any body improve so fast. He also thinks six months will do me. As to experience and a knowledge of the Indians, that time will make me as familiar as a year would, for I am already perfectly acquainted with their customs. So you see, if Professor W—— will receive me in the fall, I will have attained all the objects of the trip, and I can return to the Academy without hurting me at all, in health or knowledge. I am very anxious to complete my education there. It would make a complete revolution in my prospects for the future to be rejected from it, although, as I said, I am now willing to enter life on my own hook. I am becoming quite an Indian; all the men here call me the little " Injun," for I shoot nearly as well as they."

He had reason afterward to modify his admiration for the Indian character; for he writes from San Antonio, October 10, 1855:

" It really seems as if we out here are living over again the life of the first settlers of Texas. The same scenes are enacted; families are being murdered by the relentless savage, whole farms are laid desolate and waste, and hardly a day passes but we hear of such a one being killed, horses being stolen, etc.

" Of course, the inhabitants protect themselves as much as possible; nearly every man who has a son able to fight has sent him out. These men have banded together, and have either stationed themselves at some point frequented by Indians, or are scouring the country. In this way some few savages have been killed, and horses recovered from them. But the savage is bent on revenge, and he has it. Just as certainly as one savage is killed, his death is revenged by the inhuman butchering and slaughtering of five innocent women and children. The details of some of these murders are horrible. . . . .

"If I was not away from home so far, I would certainly join a company and go out. My indignation has been aroused, and my patriotism called upon, and at this moment I am willing to sacrifice my life for the country.' This is not bravery, when you are all safe in the house ; but I mean what I say, and if I had the chance, I would carry it out."

A vein of pleasantry crops out occasionally in his home letters, as in this :

"As to letting you decide my marriage (if ever) for me, I don't know about it. 'Agreeable girl,' just suits me. 'Old man worth a quarter of a million ; palace on Fifth

Avenue ; cottage on Hudson :' all right, as to my temporal interests ; but as to my spiritual needs, how is it ? However, I shall consider it, on my return."

More characteristic of him is the thoughtful religious turn that appears in the following :

"You are pleased to know that I think often of my mother. Truly, then, you will often be pleased; for she is, and shall always be, thought of by me. I was her first-born and your first hope. May I ever think of her who is no more, and honor him who yet lives! What a glorious thought! My mother is an angel! and angels are with God! We were never worthy of her when on earth, and are we now? Who can tell? Ask your conscience; it says, No! You say I will be to-morrow; but ' no man knoweth the hour when the Son of man cometh!' Could you bear the idea that your lost one was in heaven, and you an outcast?"

Only the most earnest, filial, and Christian love could promote a lad of fifteen to such fidelity of appeal.

"Before you receive this, Christmas and New-Year's will have passed, and the records of the doings of men for a year will be recorded in the Book of Life. Now is the time for new resolves; for new hopes, and new actions, victories or failures! How much I miss the family circle at this time; every thing seems dreary. My bark of life is tossed on the troubled waters of despair, and the anchor of hope alone can keep it from wrecking. But there is a good time coming!"

We do not look to a youth of fourteen for very profound or sagacious speculations upon public affairs, but the tone of Bryant's mind, both as a thinker and as a patriot, strikes one pleasantly and hopefully in some brief extracts from letters written early in 1856. Speaking of British demands, he says:

"Although I am one that would not wish that the strong and kindred ties that bind us together should be broken, still I think that the honor of our country should be maintained at all hazards. I am no half American, nor a Know-Nothing, but I am a true Democrat, as you always wished me to be. England has of late been very imperious and haughty toward us, and as a Young American, my blood boils, and my '*dander has riz*,' at their indignities.

"What has led her to act thus openly, I cannot say, unless it be that she supposes she has France for a permanent ally ; but I say, although I may be advancing a bold idea, that Louis Napoleon has not the good of England nearest his heart, and that, at the right time, he will be as anxious for her overthrow as any body."

Our hot-blooded young patriot has withal a touch of the antiquarian in his composition :

"It is natural for the American to think very little of his forefathers, and because of this, their history is lost. I have no such feelings. I reverence every thing ancient, and consider it an heir-loom never to be disposed of. The old cradle up stairs, in

4

which three generations were rocked, is invaluable to me, and if possible, shall be preserved as long as I live. I have long conceived the idea of collecting our family relics, and also of writing the history of mother's family. Aunt wants to know where the knee-breeches and buckles are that your father wore when a boy. You must not think that I am an old fogy, or that I adhere to ancient customs. I am only against the disuse of family relics, and the loss of family history."

V.

His Literary Bent.

RETURNING from Texas, in 1857, he resumed his studies at the Academy, where he distinguished himself in general literature, and in the French and Spanish languages. He had early shown a decided bent for literary composition, though his name restrained him from the customary folly of youthful poetizing—for he resolved that he would not tempt the Muses until he could feel sure of producing something worthy of the name of Bryant. His descriptive powers were excellent, and his imagination found play in romantic sketches for weekly newspapers and the lighter class of magazines.

In July, 1860, at the age of twenty, he graduated at the Free Academy, with the honor of an oration at the Commencement. His theme was "The Decline of Poesy." He lamented that "Utility is now worshiped with such devotion that the temple of Nature is deserted," that imagination is losing the vigor of earlier and simpler times, and the nobler style of poetry is slowly but surely declining. His theme was less suited to a popular assembly than to a literary club; but he acquitted himself with credit as an orator. His appearance on the stage in the Academy of Music, is quite graphically described from his own subjective point of view :

"Such a large and brilliant assemblage I have hardly seen even there. The whole scene was one calculated to excite the fortunate speakers to the highest degree of happiness. I occupied myself with my marshal's duties, and conversing with friends, until 10 o'clock, when my turn came to speak. Not without trepidation did I bow to that

large audience, and to the distinguished men
on the stage behind. But, when once started,
I went on well. I saw nothing but a confused mass of faces and gas-lights, for I
thought only of my words and gestures.
Six minutes of such pleasurable bliss as I
never before experienced, and my oration
was done. Some dozen bouquets followed
me off the stage. I expected to be nervous
and confused ; but, on the contrary, such a
vast audience to address, and such an immense building to speak in, seemed to give
me courage. I spoke in a high tone, and
my friends said they heard me well. My
speech being smooth and polished, rather
than noisy and political, did not excite much
applause, but I was satisfied with the opportunity to speak, and used my best endeavors
to do well. Never having spoken in public
before, I, of course, did not acquit myself as
well as the others."

What a beautiful commingling have we
here of youthful enthusiasm with Christian
modesty. He had already learned to " look

4*

not upon his own things" with a selfish vanity, but to look kindly upon the things of others ; not to think of himself more highly than he ought to think, but to think soberly, according to the measure that he had received from God.

Bryant's habits as a student were extremely methodical. He was systematic in his reading, and he kept all his own literary productions filed and registered with the accuracy of a man of business. He was accustomed to note personal incidents and passing thoughts in a pocket memorandum-book, and afterward to write out with care such as he deemed worthy of preservation. This practice he continued while in Texas and in the army, and among his effects are several of these little penciled journals, all carefully numbered and labeled. He was equally exact in his cash accounts.

A creditable volume might be made up of his contributions to the press. A good specimen of his powers as an imaginative writer, is the story of the romantic parentage of

Thomas-a-Becket, published in the *New York Mercury*, under the title of "The Emir's Daughter."

He mastered the French and the Spanish languages, and addressed himself earnestly to a high literary culture. His taste in art was refined. He became an adept upon the violin, and both sketched and painted with skill. His letters and journals were frequently illustrated by his pencil, and had he lived to measure his true genius, he might have made his mark either in literature or in art. But he was destined to perform a higher work than pen or pencil could execute, and to exalt a self-sacrificing patriotism above the pleasures of literature and the rewards of genius.

VI.

Growth as a Christian.

THE development of his religious character kept pace with his intellectual
growth. And he was so much a child of
the heart, that his knowledge of religious
truth seemed to be imbibed through the
affections and emotions, rather than acquired
by mental application. His faith was largely
the belief of the heart—the objective reality becoming palpable through his own inward experience. Yet it was an intelligent
faith, as calm and settled as it was earnest
and fervid.

To the eye of others, especially of those
who knew him intimately, he seemed scru-
pulously observant of religious duties, and

his letters show how deeply his mind was pervaded with the religious spirit. The tone of his piety was remarkably free and joyous. Writing to a friend who was laboring under despondency, he says : " I believe, as you know, that religion is not all sobersided ; but that you may rationally enjoy the pleasant things of life, and use them as a means of social enjoyment and physical profit. Only pray that you may be kept from evil companions and temptation, and all is right. Don't believe that you must be so sedate ; for, if you do, you will lose all the influence you might otherwise have over children to turn them to the right. Notwithstanding what you say, I believe that you have experienced the Christian's love for God more than I ; and, in fact, the expressing that feeling of doubt may be a strong proof of it. Those who affirm most loudly that they are blessed and converted are sometimes deceived. Don't for a moment doubt that you are converted ; for that would be repaying God but poorly for

His mercies ; but do your best to show that
you are, and to keep your vows to the
Church. I hope that we shall have a good
season of spiritual enjoyment when we return, and try to help each other ; and I also
pray that the coming winter may behold all
of our family enjoying the sweets of a Saviour's love."

After his graduation, the state of his
health led him again to seek a Southern
climate, and to enter for awhile upon active
business before devoting himself to special
studies for the ministry. But he found mercantile life uncongenial to his tastes, and
also, as frequently conducted, repugnant to
his principles as a Christian. After a few
months' experience in this line, he writes,
somewhat morbidly indeed, yet with a vein
of bitter truth : " Happiness cannot be found
in leaving friends for the sake of a future.
I have found to my entire satisfaction that
the attainment of wealth is, generally speaking, equivalent to serving the Devil ; and
that to bind yourself for a term of years to

a mercantile house, is to kill all the better sympathies of your nature, and to hinder your preparation for Heaven; which, after all, is the great duty of man."

And again, to his sister, he says: "I believe that this world's riches and pleasures are not the only things to look for, to labor for. Yes, Mary, I trust that I have found where the great *pearl* is; where the fountain of wealth, of love, and happiness is situated. I need not tell you where. Blessed be God, I have found it! It is at the feet of Jesus; and if God gives me grace and strength, there, and *there only*, will I look for my treasure and my happiness. Really, Mary, I never felt so happy in the love of the Saviour as I have here in San Antonio, simply because every thing has been so much against me, that I have, at last, settled my hopes on the only firm foundation. Only a a few days since I made up my mind that if God would vouchsafe me health and strength, I would devote my life to His service as a preacher of the gospel. You

know yourself that my desires and talents
lean that way, and how happy I could be
with a charge in the country, where I could
follow out my ideal of a farmer's life, and
at the same time minister to my flock. What
happiness! both for you and me! I am
sorely afraid that my insignificant body and
comparatively weak health will prevent me ;
but still the day may come yet, when I shall
be able to follow out my ideal in practice."

His fidelity to his father in a season of
business anxiety and alarm, shows how
strong he had himself become in the assur-
ance of the gospel. "You remark that my
writing you on the subject of religion has
had a salutary effect, and that you are
pleased with it, and thank me for my interest in the case. Father, when I read that
paragraph in your letter, I felt happy that
my words, written with but little hope of
effect, should have been acceptable to you.
I thank God that my prayers have at last
been answered (as I hope, by your conver-
sion) ; but if you do not yet feel in your

heart that love, which is beyond expression ; if you do not yet feel the necessity for faith in Christ, which shall carry you to heaven ; then, by all the powers of language I could use, I beseech you to delay no longer. Now, at this moment, look above the mean, sordid cares of business, and the empty show of the world, to that Saviour, who, I can testify, is able to relieve you of the burden of life's cares, and give you such a quiet, peaceful hope for the future, that you can live the true life which God intended you should live.

"Oh that I had the power to impress on both yourself and mother, the thoughts that I would utter ! but human aid is of little avail without the help of the Spirit. May you have that ! I acknowledge and believe that you have led a moral life, and that you have always hoped to be saved ; but a *merely moral* life, a *mere hope,* is not enough. You need the spirit, not the form ; and in these times of danger, trouble, and adversity—when, if you ever remember God,

5

you should now—I again ask you to think
and act on this subject.

"My heart is full, and I could fill pages,
but my natural diffidence in speaking to my
own father upon this matter compels me to
stop ; yet I know that you appreciate my
motives, and will not blame me.   As to myself, my love grows stronger the more adversity I have ; and I know full well the
force of that saying, 'What profiteth it a
man if he gain the whole world, and lose
his own soul?'   Now that millions are lost
in one hour, under your own eyes, you see
see its little use, and it must make you
think, 'of what good is it to get all this
money when I cannot take a cent with me
after I die?'   There is the point, 'after I
die,' what then ?   To you, who I know believe in a heaven, I need say no more, but
now in these times of peril, you cannot help
feeling the utter worthlessness of money, of
honor, of position.   I say that I know you
feel it ; for I feel it to its fullest extent myself, and you are much older than I am.

Since I left home I have seen the world and men in their true light ; now I see the cheat, the snares, the hollowness, the emptiness, the delusion of them all. Now, thank God! I see also that but one thing is true, and that is Heaven ; and by Divine aid I intend to let nothing hinder me from reaching it."

VII.

The Political Crisis in Texas.

THE preceding letters were written during the financial revulsion of the winter of 1860-61, when the Southern States were entering into their infamous conspiracy for the destruction of the Union. It will be remembered that young Gray set out for Texas directly after the Presidential election in November, 1860. Hardly had he arrived there when the ferment of secession began, which presently rose to a pitch that made it unsafe for an avowed patriot to remain within reach of the rebels. Hemmed in at first by business obligations, he saw little hope of escaping the impending ruin.

"We are living," he writes, "in times

such as the world never saw before, and possibly by the time this letter reaches you the most disastrous event that could happen to our beloved country, and to the lovers of liberty, will have been consummated—I mean, of course, the separation of the South from the North. Indeed, there is no doubt that before many weeks pass over our heads, I will be a citizen and a resident of a foreign country. Even now we do not live in the United States, for there is no U. S. ; and as far as oneness of country is concerned— why, I might as well be in England as to be where I am. All hope of compromise is at an end. What the future will be, peaceable or bloody, I cannot tell, but I am afraid we shall not meet again."

This was a strange and startling experience for a young man of twenty, far from home, and as yet without means or position in life.

"I started," he says, "with the brightest hopes, and God allowed me to arrive here safe. But what do I see! Our country

5*

ruined, and business at a dead stop; no hopes of reviving for months to come. Not alone these; I find myself in a place, where, to speak your sentiments is death; where it is unsafe to walk the streets; and in a place three thousand miles from home, with a good prospect of a stoppage of mails and of communication, so that I may not write you, or come back to you even. Ah, well! it will make a man of me, and I will be stronger for the conflict. Through it all I retain a lively faith in God, and to Him I look for refuge and safety. I would advise you to lay up *your* treasures in heaven."

Brief extracts from his letters in the order of subsequent events, will bring out the picture of Texan society as it appeared to an eye-witness in the winter of 1861 :

"SAN ANTONIO, *January* 19, 1861.

"One great social trouble is on account of the slaves. By some means they have become acquainted with the condition of the country, and believing that they may

eventually become free, they have been of
late very impertinent and dangerous. Numbers of them have already been arrested,
and they are not allowed to be out after
7 P. M. Some have been heard to hurrah
for Lincoln! and others have been found
with arms concealed. Two nights ago a
large haystack was burned in the centre of
the town, and a negro was arrested for
setting it on fire. A general plot has also
been discovered to burn the town and murder
their masters, to be put into effect on Sunday
the 20th inst. Believing, as I do, that it is
best for men to say little, and do their best
for the preservation of the Union at present;
why, I shall say nothing, except to express
the hope that the lovers of American liberty,
and of these United States, will finally suc-
ceed in restoring peace and prosperity to
the country. I pray for that every day, and
I know you do also."

"*January* 25, 1861.

"About a week ago, rumors began to
reach town that the 'Knights of the Golden

Circle', and various' other organizations of secessionists, were preparing to make a descent upon San Antonio, in order to capture the arsenals and the Government stores. These men were without authority from the State or from the people, and therefore the citizens of San Antonio were apprehensive that if they came they would attempt to plunder and take advantage of the times. You know how many lawless men there are in Texas who would gladly join such an expedition for the chance of making something out of it, and you can imagine, therefore, why the citizens, in common with V. & B., should have some fears for the safety of their lives and their property. On the receipt of the news of the coming of this force of twelve hundred men, the town was thrown into the greatest confusion. Negro insurrection and every thing else was forgotten, and every one began to prepare by arming himself and his house.

" General Twiggs expressed his determination to resist the taking of Government property by any mob of lawless men, and he was also authorized by the Governor to protect the arsenal, etc. He therefore armed the United States troops here, sent out scouts, and also sent for more soldiers from the forts above. The Common Council held a special meeting to discuss matters, and this morning the result of their conference is seen in a notice, posted all around the streets, saying that : ' Whereas, the unsettled condition of the times, and the danger of an attack,' etc. ; ' we therefore order the citizens to assemble at 10 A. M., and enroll themselves into companies, as a protection to the city.'

"General Twiggs has also placed troops at the disposal of the Mayor, and they are to act in concert. Special police have been sworn in, and, indeed, the streets have been patrolled by troops and citizens for some time past. A company is forming this morning to protect property in the vicinity of V. & B.'s store, who have their headquarters in Mr. Eagar's new store, next door

to us. A portion of the force was expected
last night, but it did not come. Well, the
gist of the matter is this, that many men in
the State wish to take the arsenals and forts
before secession, and those are the ones,
joined with some who come for plunder,
whom we expect to attack us.

"Then, again, there is another party who
wish to keep the State in the Union as long
as possible, and who also will resist any
mob of secessionists until the vote of the
people has declared that the State shall
secede. Of such men are Sam Houston,
General Twiggs, Vance & Brother, and most
all of the merchants, of course ; for, in case
of the withdrawal and disruption of the
Federal power and troops in Texas, the
Indians will entirely sweep the frontier, and
even now, the country is in a great state of
alarm from their frequent depradations.
The State has no money in the treasury,
and cannot get any ; and if secession takes
place, as of course it will, then every man
will have to be for himself. Merchants will

be ruined, and the State will be put back
many years in her progress."

"*February* 2, 1861.

" By yesterday's mail we received news
of the secession of Louisiana on the 26th
of January. This news destroyed the hopes
of the Union's preservation in the minds of
the Union lovers, but the secessionists were
in great glee over it ; and there is no doubt
but that it will influence the action of
Texas.

" The Convention to consider this subject
is now in session at Austin, and the latest
reports show that it will, and in fact has
passed the ordinance. Sam Houston, who
all along has been in favor of holding back,
is now affirmed to have turned around, and
is strong for immediate secession. The action of the Convention has, however, to be
submitted to the people, about February
23d, so that the result will be known by
the 4th of March. The people may decide
against secession, as the Union feeling is
very strong in Texas, but that is uncertain.

General Twiggs is ready to give up his troops in that event, and most of the United States officers are ready to leave for their native States when he does so."

"*February* 16, 1861.

"In my last to you I said that Texas had been declared to have "seceded" by the Convention. Well, since that date all has been quiet, but I knew that it only foreboded a storm; and sure enough, I woke up this morning, and found that some five hundred men, K. G. C.'s, had come into town about daylight, had taken the *Alamo*, and were assembled ready to take the United States troops and Government property, peaceably or otherwise. Of course, we were all in a great state of excitement; for the streets were full of armed men, both on foot and on horseback, prepared to fight desperately. I buckled on my pistol and went out about 6½ o'clock, and found the house-tops and all available places taken possession of by the militia, so as to resist. During this time, a consultation was being held between General Twiggs and the other officers, to decide whether to give up the Government property to the militia, or to resist. Every moment we expected the fight would commence. V. & B. closed the store, and got their shooters ready ; so did the other merchants.

" The main plaza was guarded by troops of Rangers from other parts of Texas, and the side streets leading to the arsenal and Vance's Government-buildings were guarded by K. G. C.'s and city troops. The city militia was called out, and I got ready to go also ; but I at last concluded to stay and defend V. & B.'s store. Well, so passed the morning ; a fight seemed inevitable ; families left town, stores closed up, and every man armed himself. But, about 12 o'clock, a shout announced that the consultation was ended, and that General Twiggs had given over the Government property to the State. So the militia took possession, and the rest disbanded. At my my present writing, all is quiet again, but

6

how long it will be so I don't know ; for General Twiggs has been discharged from command here, and Colonel Waite has been appointed by the Secretary of War. The colonel will be here in a few hours, and he may make mischief again. The city is, of course, full of strangers, drunken and lawless, and we fear trouble from them ; but we are prepared. The United States troops here, to the number of one hundred and fifty, will leave in a few hours for the San Pedro Springs, where they will camp and wait for Colonel Waite to take command of them. They will march for the coast soon with their arms, and leave, I suppose, for New York. Well, so I have seen a revolution, and passed unharmed. Five men were accidently shot this morning."

It was now apparent, that, with his love for the Union and his manly love of liberty, young Gray could not long remain in this hot-bed of treason. He writes, on the 20th of February :

" Suffice it to say, that most of the time I

have had to carry a pistol, and when I have written most of my letters here I have had a pistol by me on the desk. As you might also know, I *dare* not express any senti‐ments against secession for fear of taking the penalty, and I am also afraid to write to you, or any one else, a true account of the state of society here ; for it is a fact, they open the letters of any person who is at all suspected."

He would have left at once for the North, but was prevailed upon to wait a few weeks longer in order to escort a lady relative. How critical was his position appears from the following note of March 2 :

" I shall do my best to choke down my disgust, my fears, and my contempt for the movement now going on here, until Mrs. V. is ready to go to New York, which, at the furthest, I hope will not be more than three weeks, and then I pray God to speed me on my journey home ; for my blood boils with indignation at the tyranny I see here daily—at the starvation, and the many acts consequent upon a revolution. Yet, I cannot, I dare not speak a word for fear of the rope ; and they say that letters are violated in the post-office. But, for once, I will speak out, and if any of the self-assumed committees see this, they can do as they please, only may God have mercy on them !"

The following estimate of the value of secession to Texas, written in March, 1861, has been sadly corroborated by the events of the war :

" You ask me now, What has Texas gained by secession ? I answer, Nothing ! absolutely nothing ! She has lost the Overland Mail, Pacific Railroad, and the immense yearly expenditures of the United States Army. With her own hands she has poured forth her own life-blood, and spurned from her midst the very source of her wealth.

" Besides this, she has brought upon herself a calamity more to be dreaded than a pestilence. I refer to the Indians, who, emboldened by the departure of the United States troops from the long line of our frontier, are now desolating it with all the savage ferocity of their nature.

"Day after day we receive news of the murdering of whole families, and the stealing of thousands of horses and cattle from the poor settlers. The frontier is almost depopulated, by reason of the desertion of its inhabitants, and is now entirely at the mercy of the redskins. They have even been so bold as to come within five miles of this large town. The cry for aid and protection has, of course, been responded to by the people of San Antonio; young and old, rich and poor, have left their business, and are scouring the country. Your correspondent would also have gone, could he have gotten a horse.

"More than this; the Mexicans along the Rio Grande, knowing of the revolution, are about to prey on us; and Cortinas, the outlaw, is now upon the frontier, with some six hundred bandits, waiting, they say, for a chance to plunder."

"With the scarcity of money, and the

6*

prospective tariff, we shall suffer much here, unless a kind Providence gives us a bountiful harvest.

"If I mistake not, the tyranny and oppression of the Convention at Austin, must soon produce its effect, and before long you may expect to hear of great uprisings of the people here in Texas, as well as throughout the South. To conclude: Texas, by her hasty action, has sunk to the position which she occupied ten years ago."

Though the terrorism of rebel rule has prevented any general uprising of the Unionists in Texas, there are thousands of loyal men yet in that State, anxiously awaiting its liberation by a Union army.

A few weeks before, Bryant, in company with a Methodist minister, had visited the mountains of the Guadalupe, traveling on horseback, with such accoutrements for camping out, as two mustangs could carry. On the fifth day, having exhausted their supply of food, the travelers missed the trail, which had been covered by snow-

drifts, and at nightfall came to the fearful
conviction that they were lost. Bryant's
account of this adventure, written for the
Evening Post, after his return to New York,
may serve also for a picture of the disap-
pointment and disaster which had over-
taken his young life by reason of the storm
of rebellion that swept over the State of his
adoption :

. . . . " Our attention being dis-
tracted by the many deer that bounded
across our path, blinded us to the fact that
we were wandering hither and thither ; and
only when the thick gathering shadows
compelled us to lead our stumbling steeds,
did we awake to the reality of our being
lost.

" Lost ! Yes ; and the last ray of light
departed ; leaving us, on this barren peak,
alone to our bitter musings. It was impossible to proceed ; deep ravines lay beyond
and at the side of us ; yet how could we
pass the night in such a spot ?

" The wind had freshened, and was blow-

ing so piercing cold that, hastily gathering
up some bits of wood, we built a fire, by
the light of which we staked out our ponies to feed as best they might on the scanty
crisp grass.　Heaping branches on the fire,
we soon had a roaring blaze, and clearing
away the stones, we spread our blankets on
the ground, placed our saddles for pillows,
and with our feet to the fire, essayed to
sleep.　But, with shaking limbs and chat-
tering teeth, we could not woo the 'sweet
restorer,' and to add to our discomfort, a
fear of surprise and capture by Indians
haunted us with all its terrors.　Every
sound or stamp of our horses' feet was to
us the coming of the savage foe ; every
rushing of the wind, his stealthy advance.
And thus, hour after hour of almost insup-
portable nervous agony passed slowly by,
until, in very despair, we destroyed the
source of our little warmth, that it might no
longer be a beacon to the enemy.　As I
stood peering into the darkness, the full
moon rose, and by its light I glanced at

my watch. It was midnight of the 31st of December, 1860.

" See! what form is that speeding across the misty moonbeams, and plunging into the dim shadows beyond? 'T is the Old Year seeking its rest! Now comes the young giant, son of Mars! The battle-year has dawnèd!

" Thus did I pass that New-Year's Eve— a shivering sentinel on the mountains of the Guadalupe!

" Many moments did we stand there, quiet as nature around, thinking of the loved ones at home, and conjuring up gloomy visions of the future, so soon to bring true our wildest fears. But the chilling wind of the mountain top compelled us to descend to the bottom of the nearest ravine; where, with some dead trees, we again made a fire, around which we passed the remainder of the night, anxiously awaiting the break of day. As the first streak of gray light appeared we ascended to the peak, gathered our trappings, saddled and mounted, and when the sun rose were seeking to find some way of descent into the valley.

" By dint of much labor in riding and leading our ponies, we reached the prairie, in which, after many disappointments, we found a stream whose course we determined to follow, in hopes of meeting with a settlement either that day or the next. Heart-sick and dispirited, weak with hunger and exposure, we rode listlessly on until noon had come and gone, but no human habitation was to be seen. Oh, happy sight! Oh, glorious reality! For in the distance a thin column of smoke went curling up into the air. With vigor now in every limb, we whipped and spurred until the long looked-for cabin came in view, and we were soon making our ' New-Year's call.'

" The German bachelor exile was most happy to see us, and politely invited us ' to step into the back parlor and take a little something to eat ;' which we did to our great satisfaction and considerably to his loss. The next evening, January 2, 1861, as we gained the ridge of a rise of ground, we beheld the many glittering lights of the Cindad of San Antonio de Bexar.

"I need hardly tell how, subsequently, I was obliged to leave the scenes of my adventures, and return to the loved fireside from which I now write, nor why I am about to join the ranks of the army for the Union. My companion but recently took a horseback tour for the airing of his political opinions, across the great Indian territories, from Texas to Iowa, and now will pass a Happy New-Year in a free land.

"I bless God for his mercies! I thank him for his guidance! But I pray to be preserved from passing another New Year's on the mountains of the Guadalupe."

VIII.

Enlisted for the War.

LEAVING San Antonio on the 4th of
April, 1861, he returned to New York
by way of Alabama, Georgia and Tennessee,
barely escaping the embargo which the rebel
leaders placed upon emigration to the North.
His soul was so fired with patriotism that
he would have enlisted at once as a private,
if his health had been equal to the service.
He went so far as to offer himself to the
medical examiners, but was refused as want-
ing in physical stamina.

His friends urged him to prepare himself
for the ministry—a work for which he had
a special aptitude. But while he longed
thus to honor Christ, he shrank from an

(72)

office so responsible and so sacred, through a feeling of personal unworthiness; and besides, he was ready "to sacrifice that also for his country." At the same time, in the depressed state of business, there seemed to be no opening in commercial or in literary pursuits congenial to his tastes. Months afterward, while holding an honorable position in the army, referring to this period of uncertainty, he said:

"It seems a touch of romance, or rather is it not a good Providence that has led me! When in the winter of 1860 in Texas, I suffered so much from fear of the malignant traitors there, I wondered if ever I should occupy any decent position in life again; and then this winter also, when I almost despaired of obtaining any employment, and actually ·taught school at one dollar per week, I hardly believed that my present good fortune would ever come; although I did sometimes have the temerity to dream that I might get into the Union army as an officer. You and father never knew, in

7

those few despairing months for me, how often I left the house for the express purpose of enlisting as a private in some regiment ; and many times did I stand before the door of a recruiting office ready to sign the rolls, but *something* held me back. I prayed earnestly for guidance in my troubles and my course. As the result of God's care, I am now in Washington, in (may I not say it) the responsible and honorable position of Aid to General Doubleday."

So resolute was he for entering the army in some capacity, that when refused as a private, and induced by his father to seek health and quiet in the country, he "could hear nothing but the long-roll call for men to fall in and join the great Army of Freedom." Restless and discontented under his enforced quietude, he started to walk the distance of a hundred miles from Dover Plains to New York, with a view to hardening himself for the fatigues of a campaign. He then commenced to drill and to study tactics under Colonel Tompkins, and in a

short time was able to stand his examination
as a line officer. In the month of December,
1861, he received a commission as First
Lieutenant in the Fourth New York Heavy
Artillery, and soon after took his departure
for the seat of war. The consecration of
such a youth to such a cause is most fitly
described in these lines from the patriot and
poet whose name he bore :

"NEW. YORK, *March* 8, 1864.

"MY DEAR SIR—I am very glad that you
are about to give the world a memoir of
Bryant Gray. The example of this young
man's amiable and blameless, and at the
same time active and useful life, will, I am
sure, suffer nothing in your hands. I have
always taken an interest in his personal
history from the time that his father, with
whom I had no previous acquaintance, informed me, while his son was yet an infant,
that as a token of his regard for me, he had
given him my name. It gave me pleasure
to hear from time to time of his progress as
a scholar, and of the unfolding beauty of his

character.   Most particularly was I glad to
learn, that to a spirit more than commonly
adventurous, he joined a singular innocence
of life and tenderness of conscience.   When
he entered on the career of a soldier, the
thoughts which arose in my mind I have
since expressed in the verses which follow :

" Youth who hast left the household roof
    Yet uncorrupt and innocent,
And brought thy virtue to the proof
    That waits it in the soldier's tent,

" Think that the cause is half divine
    That girds thee with the warrior's brand,
And be the steadfast purpose thine
    To wield it with a stainless hand.

" Then shouldst thou perish in the strife,
    The tears that weep thy death shall flow
For one who gave a stainless life
    To shield his country from the foe.

" Or when the storm of war is stilled,
    Tears warm and soft as summer rain
Shall welcome him who, from the field
    Brings back a life without a stain.

"But these lines very imperfectly express the influences which preserved the purity of this excellent young man's character. He had submitted himself humbly to the teachings of Jesus, and putting his trust in the Divine aid, which is vouchsafed to all who seek it in sincerity, and affectionately contemplating the life which the Great Doer of Good passed on earth, he sought to make that life the model of his own, and to engage others in like manner to imitate it. I rejoice that a life so pure and happy, from its beginning to its close, is to have a worthy record, and to be commended by you to the study of the young men of our country, who, like the subject of your memoir, have left the shelter of their homes for the toils and temptations of the camp.

"I am, dear sir, faithfully yours,

WM. C. BRYANT.

"Rev. Dr. J. P. THOMPSON."

IX.

The Soldier and his Home.

LIEUTENANT GRAY began his military career among the defenses of Washington, where his regiment was stationed. Here, at first, he had the simple routine of a line officer within fortifications, with none of the excitement of a campaign. But he contrived to give variety and zest to camp-life by his practical efforts for the welfare of his men, and by a constant and lively correspondence with friends at home. A New York paper of January 20, 1862, reported on the authority of a visitor to the army, that "Lieutenant Gray, of First Regiment Heavy Artillery, now at Fort Richmond, wants books and tracts. He goes around himself and gathers them up from any quarter he can, to distribute among his men."

About the same date he wrote to a friend : " We started a temperance pledge in our company the other day, and many have signed it, including myself. We have also a society that agrees to kick every man who swears in the barracks ! But, of course, the future alone will show what can be done in these things."

I find no report of the effect of this application of "muscular Christianity" to the vice of swearing ; but it were well to have some method of stamping profaneness as vulgarity. It is evident that Lieutenant Gray lost nothing in the favor of his men by taking high ground for morality and religion, for subsequent events proved him to be a most popular as well as efficient officer. At the same time his home letters were full of affectionate, minute, and playful interest in the affairs of his household. To a little sister he sends this amusing message :

" I am glad that A—— has yet so much life about her that she likes to play with the kitten ; but tell her that she must not play all the time. When mother calls her to do something, she must softly put the kitten in a drawer and lock it up, so that it won't be running around and distracting her attention ; then, when she is through with her work, she can play with the kitten again. She might have an india-rubber pipe run from inside the drawer out through the window, so that the kitten can get some air and not smother."

Again, he writes to her :

" Your little letter to me was very welcome, and I hope you will write me again. I am glad that you write so well ; and now that you go to school, I suppose that you will soon write as well as Mary or Amelia. But do not spend too much time with your cat in playing, for then you cannot study as you should. I hope that I shall come back soon, for I would like to see you again, and I often think of you.

"Well, I have but little time to write to-night, and to-morrow I am to go on a journey, so I must bid you good-by for the present. Of course, you will write me again, and remember to pray for us all every day, and love your Saviour."

To another sister who was beginning to cherish hope in Christ, he sends his maturer counsels :

"WASHINGTON, *April* 17, 1862.

" I am sorry that you cannot find any one to talk with about the Saviour as familiarly as you desire. Indeed, I wish I were with you for a few hours, and could converse and sing as we did out on the hill last summer ; but you know I must now sacrifice many things to the cause of my country. But I am certain that if you will only throw off your timidity and bashfulness, you will find many glad to talk or pray with you. Father, also, I know, would like to have you speak with him on the subject of religion ; and I wish you would do so, and pray for him and for mother, and for all of us, as often as you

can. Still, even if you cannot find any one
to talk with, you know you always have the
Saviour himself; He will always listen to
you; and oh, how gladly he accepts the love
of a young heart like yours!"

And again, writing to the same, he
says:

"Your remarks about the Sunday-school
are made in the right spirit, and I hope you
will never get tired of it. It is very true
that many girls think they are too large to
go to Sabbath-school, but I know you do
not. What more pleasant place is there,
with sweet singing, and love beaming from
every face! Then to be a teacher, as I
know you will be, if you live to be a few
years older—what joy to teach those glorious truths, and to lead some little child to
the Saviour!"

He himself knew the pleasure of leading
children to God through the Sabbath-school,
though he never knew in this world how
much good he had accomplished. While
residing in New York, on his return from

Texas, he taught a mission school in a poor district on the western side of the city, and was very active in bringing street-boys into the school. Recently, his father, ordering some goods from a grocery, gave his name and number to the clerk, who on hearing them exclaimed, with surprise and pleasure, " Oh, I know that house, Lieutenant Gray lived there! He was the making of me. He found me one Sunday playing with wicked boys on the street ; he coaxed me into his Sunday-school ; he followed me up through the week ; he got me my place ; he took me to his house to talk with me ; he made me what I am. I loved him as my best friend, and when he died I mourned for him as for a brother."

The spiritual good of his own family always lay near his heart, and he lost no opportunity of furthering this, either by conversation or by letter. To a younger brother with whom he had had faithful conversations at home, he writes (May 5, 1862) :

" Well, I have written you a long letter ;

you must write me a good one in answer. I
hear that you have been quite sick, but I
hope you are well now. Oh! my brother,
don't neglect to pray, and love your Saviour
with all your heart. How happy you will
be always if you do that! God bless and
make you a good and dutiful son and scholar
and a faithful Christian!"

His filial affection was remarkably strong.
He always confided in his father's counsels,
and doted upon him as his dearest friend.
How touchingly is this expressed in the
following lines, and how beautiful, too, the
analogy of this filial devotion to the confidence of Christian faith. He writes to
his father (April 11, 1862):

" I am happy to think that you consider
all my letters interesting because they
come from your son. The simple certainty
that I *have* a father who follows my foot-
steps with such anxiety and pleasure as I
know you do, is a pleasing thought to me,
and helps sustain me in the many dark
thoughts which I sometimes have of the fu-

ture. I only wish, and God knows how I pray for it, that both you and I may look upward to our mutual Father in heaven, and love and thank him for his care and mercy!"

The minute interest of the soldier in his home circle should be reciprocated by them in their letters to the camp. Such letters should abound in familiar domestic details, and be always full of hope and good cheer. The practical hints of the following should be regarded by all families having representatives in the army. Writing to a sister, Bryant says :

"Aware of the truth of your remark that home-life is not so varied as one might suppose, I have also to add that when one is away, especially situated as I am, every item, even to the most minute and seemingly unimportant, is of great import and value. Therefore, please bear this in mind hereafter, and keep me well posted, even as to whether you take dinner at 1 or 6 o'clock; or whether Margaret says 'parrot' to Alice, etc.

" I only wish, sometimes, that I could change my identity for a day or so, or in some way see myself and my actions as I know you must observe them at home. For instance, when I stood guard that lonely night, it was romance and hardship both to me ; but I know it must seem much more romantic to you."

Still, with all the romance of war, and with all his conviction of duty, his heart often yearned for home. Thus he writes from Washington, April 23, 1862, to his Sister Mary .

" For some reason best known to Providence, my life seems destined to be spent away from home. Scarcely do I get there, than some unexpected turn of events calls me away. I grant that this educates me to a better appreciation of the world, and the ways of its many inhabitants. From being as I once was, a boy of an exceeding modest and retiring disposition, it has made me a *man*, with higher aims, and I trust nobler purposes. From being microcosmatic, it has made me cosmopolitan in my tastes and desires ; but with all this, I fear that the spirit of unrest is gaining ascendency over me, that I can no longer be satisfied with the quiet of home ;—a disposition to move and keep moving, and a love for excitement, which will not be satisfied by the monotony of ordinary business routine. I say that I fear all this—it is but a natural consequence, yet I will not give way to it. That love for my fireside, which is so deeply implanted in my breast, that pleasure which I have in the nearness of a *true* friend only there to be found, will and must be the power which shall hold me, till God, in His great mercy, shall end this War for Freedom, and take me safely to your side once more."

X.

As a Staff Officer.

LIEUTENANT GRAY'S efficiency as an officer, his general intelligence, and his high moral tone soon attracted the attention of his superiors, and in February, 1862, after only a few weeks of military service, he was assigned to a position on the staff of Brigadier-General Doubleday. The following letter exhibits both his soldierly pride and his manly modesty in view of the promotion. It was written to his father from Washington, March 5, 1862:

"I thank my friends for their congratulations, and to some extent I agree with you, when you say, that I will find others of less merit occupying higher places. I am much afraid, however, that I have been too highly estimated by General and by Major Double-day. I would rather be under-estimated and rise gradually, than to fall suddenly.

" But this position has been thrust upon me without my consent or knowledge, and if I do not come up to the General's expectations, of course the fault will be his own. I am glad that you attribute my success to the right cause. I sincerely hope that now you will seek for that religion which can alone sustain and comfort you in these times. My example may be of no value, but your own future welfare depends on the choice you now make. Won't you take the step and taste of the happiness, peace and joy that flow from it ?"

With respect to the feeling of his regiment at parting with him, he adds :

" The fact of my always doing my duty to my men, attending to all their wants, and being kind and affectionate toward them, has made them love me, and they really overwhelm me with their kindness. But I must not flatter myself any more.

8*

Pride always has a. fall, and I shall still continue to pray God to keep me an humble Christian."

His staff-position brought him nearer to the heart of the war. He entered upon it at the critical period when General McClellan, having brought the Army of the Potomac to the highest perfection of drill and organization, was about to try its efficiency in the Peninsular campaign against Richmond. For a time Lieutenant Gray was detained in Washington and its vicinity, but he was soon called to active service in General McDowell's corps. The insight into the spirit of army officers, and his familiarity with affairs at Washington, revealed to him much of that ambiguous patriotism and conditional loyalty which subsequent events, and the publication of contemporary documents, have now laid bare to the public. Probably at no time in the history of the war has there been so much of military *dilettanteism* and so little of moral enthusiasm in the high places of the army.

He writes from Washington, April 5, 1862 :

" I have a slight presentiment that I will not see home and you all again, but still we can but trust in God, and hope to meet elsewhere. I still have hope of the speedy termination of the war, but my belief is somewhat shaken by my observation of the many traitors in the army."

His letters abound in praise of the loyalty and the capacity of his own General, but his insight into the tone of the army, led him to write : " I tell you, father, I see clearly that through Providence and the valor of our soldiers alone can we defeat rebeldom. Treason, incompetency, and bad generalship are so prevalent, that it seems as if the country must be turned upside down to make it even partially clean and pure. But I believe God is with us !"

His criticisms may have been too severe. But his faith in our cause sustained him under all these outward discouragements. In reply to his father's exhortation to personal bravery, in view of an impending battle, the

Lieutenant expresses feelings worthy of the true soldier :

"I grant that my temperament may be a nervous one, but in a great cause like this, my principles are firm, and I know that in the rush of battle the very excitement will make me cool and quiet—it always does. I certainly shall try (as you hope I will) to do my duty as one who means it, and I thank you for your hope that I may, after all is over, return safely home.

"I must say here, that my love for my country is as strong as ever, but unfortunately the breaking down of all my prejudices in favor of the generals, officers, and leading men of our army and country makes me fear for our future. Could you but see, as I do now, the *concealed* treason of many high in authority, and the absolute disavowal by them of their oaths to attend to the best interests of the nation, you would feel anxious for coming days also."

Perhaps the Lieutenant's judgment of his superiors was warped by his own zeal for freedom. Yet the fact will not be questioned, that the reluctance of many officers to favor the enfranchisement of the negro, was for a long time an incubus upon the army. Conditional loyalty could never inspire heroic deeds. But that day of darkness and doubts has passed away.

A little later, just starting from Washington for the front, Bryant writes to a sister:

"I am sorry to say that I find life in the army not conducive to the 'higher Christian experience,' and I am not so sensitive and deeply religious as before. I am glad to see that you have gained so high a standpoint. Struggle on! pray for me, and for us all, and if I should not come back to you, I hope we will (I dare not say *I* will) meet in heaven.

"I think, from what I hear, that we will have much fighting (if the enemy don't back out), and I expect before long to be in Richmond. I may not have much chance to write you when we get to marching, but I shall write, if possible, from Fredericksburg, and as often as I can afterward. If you look in the papers closely for any action in which General McDowell's *corps d'armée* and General Doubleday's brigade are concerned, you will see of course if any accident happens to me, or any of us. I shall always, if need be, uphold my country's flag, and be no dishonor to you and my family."

The campaign into which he now entered for active service tested all his faith and fortitude. It was soon apparent that his physical strength would be severely tasked by its exposures. Writing from camp, opposite Fredericksburg, about the middle of June, he says:

"Since the 12th I have had a sick time of it—in bed all the time; but to-day I am much better and stronger. Doctor says I came very near having a bad type of typhoid fever. But I have had bilious fever, headache, and diarrhœa all together. So now I am, of course, pretty weak, as I have eaten nothing for some days. I am lying in my bed, raised up on my elbow. In a day or two, at the outside, I shall be around, and at work, as all danger has passed.

"I am sorry that I have no public religious privileges, for without sympathy and co-operation with others, we become cold and lax in discipline. The negroes around, of whom we employ quite a number, are, however, quite lively; and their singing in the evening of old-fashioned Methodist hymns is quite refreshing. I shall strive, however, to keep close in my thoughts to God, and to you all, and hope for the coming time when I can enjoy worship in New York."

Just as he had recovered from this illness, his constant forebodings of disaster from the Peninsular campaign, were more than verified in the retreat upon Harrison's Landing.

"*July* 3, 1862.

"I assure you that the Senators and the people are waking up to the fact that a new policy must be adopted, other than conciliation, before the war can be ended. Every

one here is asking for the news from McClellan ; nothing—dark—defeat is the whisper.
There is no doubt that McClellan is defeat-
ed, and you will please remember my letter
to you some time in April, describing what
would be the inevitable result of his going
down to the Peninsula. Defeat, I said ; defeat it is ; and what a terrible loss of life.
Really, it seems as if every household in the
land was to be smitten with the ' death of
its first-born.'   But I think all is for the
best, for more troops have been called for,
and we can crush with greater power."

"*July* 5, 1862.

"If our fortunes are retrieved, and we
can outnumber the rebels, Richmond may be
taken, and the war carried into the more
central portions of the South. But now I
tell you the crisis is at hand, and God alone
knows what the result will be. I cannot
believe that He will desert us in this cause,
which seems to be, and *is*, so just and holy.
But I do think that Providence is chastising
us for our sins, and forcing us by bitter suf-

fering to the adoption of a policy which will
be consistent with religion, humanity, and
justice toward our fellow-men and ourselves.
I could give you incidents, witnessed by my
own eyes, at the relation of which, you would
wonder that we have succeeded as well as
we have. We can only hope that an over-
ruling Power, and the strong common sense
and patriotism of the Northern people will
bring us out right. But, I fear, you will
think me a politician, so I will restrain my
wrath and just indignation."

9

XI.

General Pope's Campaign.

THE appointment of General Pope to the supreme command in central Virginia, revived the hopes of the nation, which had been dispirited by the delays and disasters of the Peninsular campaign; and his announcement of a vigorous and aggressive warfare, though made in terms of unmilitary extravagance, cheered the army already weary of the " conciliatory" method of dealing with the enemy. It was not then foreseen that he and his army must be sacrificed to the necessity of extricating General McClellan's army from the Peninsula. On the eve of marching, Lieutenant Gray wrote from Fredericksburg, to his father (at the close of July, 1862):

"I wish to warn you not to believe any of the monstrous stories they fabricate about the defeat of the Union army and the success of the rebel cause. You will no doubt be almost forced to believe that we have given up the contest and all is lost! But don't credit it at all. We are now in a better condition than ever before; the people have waked up to the fact that we are at war, and now demand a policy for, and a conduct of it, which shall crush the rebellion speedily. In answer to this call of the people, the President and Congress have made the 'Confiscation Act' a law; the slaves of rebels are freed, the soldiers subsist upon the enemy, and shoot guerrillas; in fact, in every way, except universal emancipation is not yet proclaimed, has the policy been changed for the better. Yes, the past has been dark, and a few weeks since it did, indeed, look as if our cause was almost ruined. But, thank God! a vigorous policy is now in operation."

In the hope inspired by this new phase of

the war, though scarcely recovered from a
debilitating illness, Lieutenant Gray entered with ardor and alacrity upon the
march to the front. His description of the
marching and fighting in that brief but
terrible campaign under General Pope,
would furnish a valuable chapter in the history of the war. But there is room here
for only a few extracts:

"CULPEPPER C. H., *August* 13, 1862.

"On our way we heard the roar of the
cannon from the battle-field at this place,
and it moved us to march faster. But such
suffering for water! the day was intensely
hot, the road dry and dusty, and no water
to be found, except at long intervals, and
then dirty and warm. Finally, we came to
the Rapidan River. We had just been
drenched to the skin in a severe storm, and
were in no humor to wade through the river,
which was stomach deep; but in the men
went with a shout, and then on the opposite
bank we bivouacked. The heat and dust, and
lack of water, had, however, caused the men

to fall down by the wayside in such numbers, that, when we camped, each regiment
numbered only about one hundred and fifty
or two hundred men. The wagon-train
was also far behind, stuck in the mud, and
the men suffered for want of provisions. A
dispatch soon came from General McDowell
ordering us to leave camp before daylight,
put the men's knapsacks into the wagons,
and join him with all possible speed. So
General Doubleday gave orders for us to
take a little sleep, and to start at 2 A. M.
All night stragglers were coming in, and
wagons also, so that we slept but little.
I lay on a board bench, but at 1 o'clock A.M.,
the General sent me into the camp to wake
the cooks, and have the coffee and meat for
the men. At 2 A. M. the staff mounted,
and by the clear moonlight I helped form
line in the road. Major D. led the ad-
vance-guard, the soldiers loaded their pieces,
and the word was given, ' Forward !'
Slowly through the dense woods, with our
scouts watching, and no noise (save from a

few wagons), we marched till daylight, when we came up with General Patrick's brigade in camp at a cross road. We halted to await the arrival, by another road, of General King's division. Presently they came—regiment after regiment of infantry, cavalry and artillery, and soon we started, acting as rear-guard to the division. A section of artillery was given us, and away we went. The men being lightened of their heavy burdens, and the roads being moist, we marched splendidly, but it waxed warm again, and as a whole *corps d'armée* was in front of us, they drank every drop of water almost, and our suffering for the want of it became intense. But still we pushed on and on. About noon we halted for an hour or so, and then in the afternoon, and into the night up to 10 P. M. we still kept on. What a sight it was to see men rush like deer for the precious water !

"I cannot describe to you the emotions which passed through my breast, while we expected every moment to hear the signal for battle. I thought of you all, and how unfit I was to enter into the presence of my Maker ; but I felt glad to fight for my country, and trusted in God's mercy. It is impossible to think that I shall not soon be in battle, for we wait for orders each moment. A kind Providence may preserve me, although my position is one which gives but little chance for life, and if I am not spared, and cannot write you again, please remember my great desire, that all of you should seek to gain God's love, and that thereby we may have a happy home in heaven."

The subsequent story how this eager advance was turned into an anxious and perilous retreat, terminating in the second disaster of Bull Run, is hurriedly told in a letter addressed to a sister then in Europe. The fatigue and exhaustion of that retreat, brought on with aggravated violence a form of disease from which the Lieutenant had suffered at Fredericksburg, and which made it impossible for him longer to ride his horse.

Accordingly at the date of this letter, we find him again in fort with his old regiment, as an officer of the line :

"Fort Ethan Allen, *Sept.* 15, 1862.

"What stores of information, and what memory-treasured sights of storied Rhine, and noble cathedrals, and grand old cities, you must have. I envy you ; and yet do you know that I love you more since I read your outbursts of patriotism and love of country, which grieved you to be away from us in this crisis, and made you feel that *you* were needed to do your share for the nation's weal ! It pays me for my sufferings and hardships to know that I have a sister who appreciates the sacrifice and loves the cause.

"After writing you from Fredericksburg, our division was ordered to march and meet the enemy. We made a forced march, and reached him, but he retreated. We advanced to Cedar Mountain, but he again advanced on us, and we were obliged to retreat, and then commenced to fight. For more than a week we fell back, and fought all the time, during which I saw my first battle, and knew what it was to hear the shells whizzing about me, and see the sad sight of men falling by me, of blood, of smoke, of ghastly wounds, and all the horrible scenes of war. Thank God! I am preserved through it all, though by many narrow escapes. But before (and only a day or two before) the retreat to Manassas, and the bloody battle there, I became so utterly prostrated and worn out by the severe marching of the fortnight previous; by the exposure of sleeping in the rain and mud; by the lack of food and of rest, and especially by the great nervous tension which anxiety and fighting produce, that I resigned my position on General D.'s staff, and, putting myself in a surgeon's hands, left for Alexandria, to rejoin my regiment, or to go into hospital. My experience and sufferings during the week it took me to get here, I can hardly describe. The rebels had got ahead of us, and destroyed the track to Alexandria, and surrounded us on every side. I almost starved, barely escaped capture, was compelled to walk many weary miles, and sleep by the roadside, and finally got on a train filled with wounded from the great battle-field, and reached Alexandria. I could not get into the crowded hospitals, and so I made my way to my regiment and company, who received me with open arms at this fort."

A letter to his father, of about the same date, gives some additional particulars of this melancholy and wearisome campaign:

"On leaving Culpepper, we advanced to the battle ground of Cedar or Slaughter Mountain, and encamped there a day or so; but the rebels advanced upon us in such large numbers that we retreated at night and made a forced march to the Rappahannock River. Scarcely had we crossed the river, when they came upon us, and a severe skirmish took place, of which I was a witness. The next day our brigade was in a severe shelling fire of the rebels; the

next day we supported a battery of light
artillery posted on the hills on one side of
the Rappahannock, while the rebels fired at
us with big guns from the other. Here we
remained for two days, the shot and shell
whizzing and singing over our heads and
about us, killing and wounding many. One
shot just grazed the blanket on my horse.
Here I first became accustomed to the sickening sight of blood and death. Suddenly
we retreated from Rappahannock Station,
and marched to Warrenton. Here we again
supported a battery for two days, with the
same horrible experience of the bursting
shell and wounds. God preserved me through
it all.

"It would be difficult," he continues, "for
me to tell you my experience in getting
from Warrenton to Alexandria. I did not
reach Alexandria until September 1, being
five days on the route. The rebels had just
burned the bridge and torn up the track in
front of us, so we had to wait for them to
be built. Finally, we had to push the cars

by hand, and at last, General Banks, who guarded the train, ordered us to leave it and walk to Fairfax Station. We defended the train up to the last moment, and then burned it. Such a time as I had you can hardly imagine—hobbling along the track, sleeping on the wet grass, and subsisting on two cups of coffee and hard bread, and a small piece of pork daily, which I begged from the half-famished soldiers. At last I reached Fairfax Station, to which the trains run from Alexandria; but here the crowds of wounded and sick soldiers from the great battle-field near by compelled me to walk some five miles more, and, after lying in a half-starved state for a day and night, I got on a train loaded with wounded, and reached Alexandria."

Major Ulysses Doubleday, who knew Lieutenant Gray both in the line and on the staff, gives the following report of his character and services, in a letter to his father:

"Upon the formation of General Doubleday's staff in March, 1862, he was appointed

Acting Aid-de-camp. His untiring and systematic industry gave the General such satisfaction that the appointment was soon made a permament one. His gentle and obliging disposition made him many friends in the command. He went with the brigade to Fredericksburg in May, and remained there until it marched early in August to join General Pope at Cedar Mountain. In July he was taken quite ill of a malarious fever, from which he had hardly recovered at the time the troops marched. He was very patient during this illness, although he suffered a great deal. The hardships he had to endure on the march to join General Pope, and afterward during the retreat of the army, were too much for him, and he resigned with a broken constitution."

To his personal bravery and his official fidelity during those memorable days, General Doubleday likewise bears this honorable testimony, in a letter addressed to his father, after the death of Lieutenant Gray:

" We all loved your son, and all felt

10

deeply grieved at his unexpected death.
While he was with us on Pope's campaign,
he always displayed the utmost alacrity in
performing every duty that devolved upon
him. He was very near me during the
artillery battles on the Rappahannock, and
I assure you my own position was any thing
but a safe one. The excessive exposure,
however, he endured on the march, the
necessity of bivouacking in the mud and
rain, the lack of food, and the irregular
nature of our meals, all contributed to injure
his constitution, and unfit him for active
service in the field. Feeling that his bodily
health was not such as to enable him to do
justice to himself or to me in the important
staff duties entrusted to him, he resigned
his commission as Aid, and resumed his
place as a line officer. I assure you I shall
ever remember him as one of the pure and
noble spirits who devoted their lives to the
great interests of humanity on this con-
tinent."

XII.

In Camp and Fort.

REDUCED again to comparative inactivity in military affairs, and forbidden by his physical condition to engage in those extra official services which had been his delight, the Lieutenant now devoted much time to the culture of personal piety in himself, and also, by correspondence, in his friends at home. In the church with which he was still connected in New York, was an association of young men, styled the "Christian Brotherhood," with which he corresponded freely upon religious subjects, especially those of a practical and experimental character. In one of his letters to the Brotherhood, he thus describes the religious disadvantages and advantages of a soldier's life:

"The great temptation here is, not to forget the great principles of religion, but to neglect to think continually of the Saviour, and to pray without ceasing. To be without a pastor or a house of worship, and no chaplain with whom to sympathize,* detracts much from one's spiritual enjoyment. Yet, even the total lack of these sweet privileges, shared in so full a measure by the Brotherhood, has a salutary effect, for it leads me to Christ. In Him I find my pastor and my companion, and in my own heart a shrine and an altar, from which to send up my incense to the Most High. It may seem anomalous to say that the life of a soldier is at all calculated to foster religious feeling, yet I truly believe it. The death of one comrade after another, and the apparent nearness of his own end, causes him to think solemn thoughts, and to lean

---

*This was written when he was separated from **his** regiment, which had an excellent chaplain.

upon the strong arm, which shall lead him to a peaceful home and eternal rest in heaven. It is thus with me, and I am a soldier. Accustomed now to the booming of cannon, the sharp rattle of musketry, and the harsh noise of war, yet my heart is not hardened ; indeed, I thank God that it is as tender as before ; my aspirations and endeavors to live the higher Christian life are as strong, and my hopes for the future glorious.

"But I should do wrong if I did not acknowledge that I am still a great sinner. The longer I live the more I feel the need of pardon, and, at the same time, my total unworthiness of such infinite mercy. Yet, working and praying, struggling and believing, will, through grace, in each of our hearts, bring about the result which we so much desire ; and then all this suffering, mental and physical, this fighting, this sickening sight of blood, and all our many tribulations, will be but as a thing of the the past, and the reality will be a meeting

10*

together, and an eternity, peaceful and serene in the presence of God."

To the same body he writes again, October, 1862 :

"Although deprived here of many comforts, especially the pleasant home fireside and church privileges, yet I feel thankful ; thankful that my life is spared ; thankful that I can serve my country, and thankful that God's mercy is even for such a sinner as I.

" We have prayer-meetings here. Last evening, in spite of the rain, we assembled in a large chapel-tent, and though the muddy ground was the only floor, the brethren knelt, and it was pleasant for us to be there. All our meetings are profitable, and yet under such circumstances of hard boards, muddy floors, and solitary candle, as might deter many city worshipers from coming. A work of grace, I believe, is going on in our regiment, and I am happy that it is. In my own heart many tares are being rooted out, and many good fruits

of those heavenly virtues, Faith, Love, and
Charity, being ripened ; yet, more than all,
I am daily learning the depths of my sinfulness, the infinite breadth of God's mercy,
and the nearness of death."

How much he prized these meetings, and
how greatly he contributed to their interest
and usefulness, his regimental chaplain testi-
fies in these emphatic terms :

"I found him one upon whom I could
rely as a man, and upon whom I could
depend as a Christian. I never knew him
to absent himself from the prayer-meeting
or from the preaching of the Word, when
in his power to attend. Indeed, he was
one of my best supports in the work I had
in hand. Some time before his death, circumstances brought him and myself under
one canvas, in the same quarter. There it
was I learned the man more fully. I found
that his mind was set upon the ministry ; he
asked me often in relation to it. He said
if he lived to get out of the army (which he
did not wish to do until the rebellion was

put down), he would make this his first business.

"I found him, for a young man, having
deep experience as to the things of God.
He carried out into practical life what he
professed—a man and a Christian at all
times and in all places."

A letter to his father, dated October 25,
1862, shows how strong was his heart in
the love of the Saviour:

"Truly, my life seems like some strange
romance, when I review it; but Providence
guides it, now as in the past, and I am sure
that the education I am receiving will be
of value to me, if—if I live. Will my religion leave me? That is the question! for
whether I live or die, it alone is *the* great
comfort and consolation. Life in the army
draws largely on one's moral strength, and
one finds but few to talk with; only the
Saviour—he is enough. But why should I
speak of deserting my God! my Redeemer!
He who takes all my sins upon himself.
No! whatever may assail, my God! my

God! I love thee with all the fervor of my heart! Do not you, too, my father?"

His Christian faith showed itself also in every new emergency of the war. Apprehending with a quick sagacity the qualities of prominent Generals, and the causes of our repeated failures in aggressive movements, he says :

"I have not for a moment doubted that God was with us. He has only been trying us ; and as we gradually root out our sins of slavery and General-worship, so fast does He give us success.

"Oh, when will our countrymen look at national affairs in a broad, patriotic, religious light? The same men who uphold General —— are bitter opponents of the emancipation policy ; and because I favor it, they call me a 'black abolitionist,' etc. But I always will stand up for Right, Liberty, and Common Sense."

Lieutenant Gray knew how to care for the comfort and pleasure of his men as well as for their spiritual welfare. On the 28th of November, 1862, he wrote :

" Yesterday, 27th, was Thanksgiving Day here also; and because I could not be at home, I got up a celebration for our company. I sent to Washington, in connection with the Captain, got several gallons of oysters, made a stew, baked beans, beef, etc., and then spread a table for the boys in a large tent. They enjoyed it hugely. In the evening I got them together in the barracks, and there we had music, singing, and speeches; made the Chaplain chairman of the meeting, and had addresses from him, the Captain, and some of the privates. Of course, I made a rousing speech! and by my jokes (inherited from you) I kept them in a roar of laughter. The meeting served to increase good feeling, and was an oasis in our desert life."

Though there was no reporter present to reflect the spirit of this feast, its impression was pleasantly recalled a year later, in a letter to Bryant's father from Orderly Sergeant Jonas McLean:

" Pardon the liberty I have taken to ad-

dress you, but I have been thinking all day
of Lieutenant Gray. How changed are all
things, from what they were last Thanksgiving ; he is in his grave, and I am at home.
The evening before Thanksgiving, last year,
he came to my tent and said he wished to
treat the company to an oyster dinner, if they
could all eat together, and wanted to know
if I could manage it so that they could. I
told him I would at all events, and bear my
proportion of the expense. No, he said, he
wished to pay the expense himself ; he had
the money, and did not know how he could
use it to a better advantage. I accordingly
got the use of the Chaplain's tent, and got
the tables ready for the whole company.
At the appointed time we all sat down, with
the Chaplain and Lieutenant Gray at the
head of the table ; and such a dinner, or a
more happy set of men, never was seen in
Fort Ethan Allen. The Lieutenant's face
fairly shone with delight, as he looked over
the tables, and saw how the boys were enjoying themselves and the day.

"It is said that 'man is the noblest work of God ;' that admitted, Lieutenant Gray was one of His master-pieces, for He has made but few like him."

XIII.

The Last Days.

THE natural feebleness of Lieutenant Gray's constitution, which from his childhood had been a source of anxiety to his friends, was in a measure counteracted by a certain elasticity of tone, derived in part from energy of will, and in part from vigorous exercise in the open air. Hence he sometimes deceived himself with regard to his physical condition, and attempted more than he was able to endure. As soon as he began to revive from the extreme and dangerous prostration induced by his service on General Doubleday's staff, his friends were cheered by the hopeful tone of his letters.

"I am now regularly on duty," he writes,

11

" although not yet well ; and here I find my-self this night writing to you in my tent, all still about me, expecting at 1 A. M. to go the grand-rounds, and visit the sentinels on the parapets in my capacity as officer of the day.

" And this is happening on the 15th of September, my twenty-third birthday! How different from the same event a year ago. But I feel proud of my position, and shall serve my country, if needs be, till my twenty-fourth birthday, if God preserves me so long."

October 9, he says : " I find myself much better, and apparently in the enjoyment of good health. The rheumatism, piles, debil-ity, etc., have left me, except weakness con-sequent upon the sickness. The weather is now so delightful, that it ought to make one feel well. I certainly look much better than I have for some time past, and am now sat-isfied that the war and campaign have not so completely broken down my constitution, as I thought they had."

"*October* 27, 1862.

"Just after finishing this letter, I succeeded in getting up nicely an extra tent, behind our other one. Although it was Sunday, I put up our little stove in it, for it was quite cold, and we felt comfortable; but soon came a pouring rain, and a high wind, which during last night increased to a perfect hurricane. Alas, for our hopes of comfort! About midnight the storm and wind blew down our stove-pipe, and then down came the tent itself, leaving us much exposed to the rain. Such a gale I have seldom seen, but this afternoon it abated, and we put up the tent again, and I now sit by the stove in it, writing you. I simply mention this to show you that my life is not entirely filled up with the pleasures of drilling, and visiting the sentinels after the hour of night."

To his father, November 11, 1862: "In fact, for a soldier, I am now quite comfortable. My tent is banked up on the sides to keep out the cold; my little cast-iron stove burns nicely; my bed, with pretty quilt from mother, looks neatly. The whole presents quite a distinguished appearance; and as I sit writing you now, on a camp-chair, the port-folio on my lap, ink-bottle on trunk, and candle on a box, I do not mind the disagreeable flapping of my tent in the wind, or the bugle, which sounds the hour of nine, for my thoughts are with you at home. I am just now thinking how glad I felt that in your letter you said that my last words to you on religious subjects caused tears of sympathy to flow, and made you thankful, that I still (even though feebly) hold to my religion. God grant that your tears may flow not at *my* poor expressions, but at the remembrance of the Saviour's sufferings for such sinners, as you and I know ourselves to be. . . . .

" Two persons who are traveling home to God certainly should not fear to express their mutual sympathies and hopes. Now, especially in this time, when the great shock of war and politics snaps asunder the bonds of friendship and love, does it behoove us to strengthen them by all the means in our power."

"*November* 28, 1862.

" I also heartily thank you for your expressions of satisfaction at my principles, and because you ask me to pray for our country, and, of course, for you. I wish prayers would save us. Alas! we have too many traitors and too much incompetency to hope for an answer to prayer, until we root out evil. But now I believe the day has dawned, and with it, and with the speedy close of the war, I hope to return to you."

The following, to his father, is of touching interest, as an exhibition of the generosity of his nature, of his cheerfulness in his work, and of hopes of health and success destined so soon to be prostrated :

"Chain Bridge, *December* 18, 1862.

" I have recently had two notes from you, the last dated 15th inst., mostly relative to a certain box, which you and Mary propose to send me. I am on the look out for it, and shall, of course, do full justice to its con-

11*

tents. What can Mary's kindness be preparing for me? Thinking now of Christmas reminds me to say, that I wish you would please honor any drafts Mary may make upon you in my name. I have directed her to make certain presents and donations, and told her to ask you for the amount needed, to be taken from my funds.

. . . . "Indeed, when I stop up the cracks in the floor and sides, which I am now doing, and shingle my roof, so that it won't wet me all over when it rains, I will have a perfect palace—that is, for a soldier. At present I have to go to the sutler for my meals, and I assure you the steep hill I have to climb to get there, adds wonderfully to my appetite. The part of the company which will be under my especial charge at this end of the bridge, still remains in the barracks at the fort, because their tents have not yet been fully pitched. To-morrow they will probably come down. Our camp is right on the rocky bank of the river, and is a forsaken ruined spot, although quite picturesque. My position makes me well known to the regiments hereabouts, and to the citizens, and is considered honorable and responsible. I am still in good health, and have good prospect of remaining so. My constant life in the open air, climbing of hills, and manual labor is the cause. But I tell you I have suffered greatly from the cold this winter in my tent, and even now, the water in my room freezes solid nearly every night. Our men are suffering much from lack of pay, now nearly six month's. There seems to be no hopes of it before next year. What is the matter? Is the Government broke?"

The following hurried note to his father was the last he penned. It tells its own story :

"SEMINARY HOSPITAL, GEORGETOWN, D. C.,
December 28, 1862.

"It pains me to inform you that the reason why I have not written to you for some days past, is a rather sudden and severe attack of pneumonia. On the 23d inst. I was well and happy as you please, but on the afternoon of that day was detailed to make a survey of the roads and houses between the Chain Bridge and Drainsville. I slept badly all that night and on getting up in the morning, found that I had a racking pain in my right breast.

"During the whole of the 24th, I was the same way, although on the 25th the pain was somewhat alleviated. I had called the doctor in, but he could not tell what the matter was, and advised me to go to this hospital for better treatment and more comfortable quarters than the regiment afforded. I did not, however, leave until Saturday the 27th, and after an excruciating ride, reached here toward evening. I found myself at once in good quarters, had good attentions, and the best medical skill; but I have not yet gained any—perhaps it is too soon to look for any marked improvement."

At first, however, no one thought him

seriously ill. His Captain says, concerning his health :

"I think he has never been really well since his campaign with General Doubleday. He was apparently very much reduced on his return, and was quite sick for some time. He thought he had fully recovered; but I think his constitution was broken down in that campaign. He spent the morning before he was taken sick with me. My wife is in camp with me ; we have our tents apart from the others. He staid until nearly 10 o'clock, and appeared as well as usual. When he left, he said he liked to visit us, as it looked like home, and we were always pleased to have him call."

On the last day of December, his father, advised by a telegram of the Lieutenant's dangerous illness, hastened to Washington, and reached the hospital at daybreak on the morning of the 1st of January, 1863. As he entered the ward where the Lieutenant was lying, the soldier, who for days had been wandering in mind, suddenly came to himself and exclaimed, " Now, there is some one here that I know! That is my father. I feel better!" Beautiful and blessed symbol of the recognition of his Father in heaven, and the joy of that knowing so soon to follow.

Chaplain Philips, of the Ninth New York Volunteers, who was kneeling at his bedside, asked him if he should pray especially for any thing. He answered, "Pray that this great distress in my left side may be removed; but if that cannot be, pray that I may have strength to endure it." Immediately he relapsed into unconsciousness, his bewildered brain all intent upon the imaginary performance of his military duties. Springing up in his bed with a preternatural strength, he would command his orderly sergeant, in a voice so loud as to be heard in all parts of the building, telling him to keep his pickets well out, as this was the first and most important duty of an officer. Once, when his father attempted to hold him back, there came another flash of recognition, and he said, "You cannot control me now, father. I am a soldier; I belong to my country."

Presently there came a lull, and his father sat quietly moistening his lips with a sponge. The soldier, as in a dream, was again a little boy standing by the bedside of his dying mother, moistening her lips, as life ebbed away. With a look of inexpressible pathos, he said, "Old memories will come back; won't they, father!" Then, springing up again in bed, with a firm voice, he ordered his men through all the evolutions of the drill, and with the command, "*Forward! march!*" he sank back into his last sleep.

A year before, he had stood "a solitary sentinel on the mountains of the Guadalupe," watching for the dawn; again, he had kept his night-watch for the New Year, a faithful sentinel, standing before the gate, until its golden hinges turned for him.

> "Lo, there!— on guard—his rank already won,
> Shining he stands, with his new armor on."

XIV.

Last Tributes.

ON Sabbath, the 4th of January, 1863, the remains of Lieutenant Gray were borne to Greenwood Cemetery, attended by a large concourse of mourners. Appropriate funeral services were conducted by the Rev. Alfred Cookman, of whose church he was a member, and by the Rev. J. P. Thompson, the pastor of his father's family. His monument bears the fitting inscription from one of his own letters:

"I do not fear the battle-field, for I look beyond it to the delights of Heaven."

Is it not among those delights that three from his dear earthly home have come for-

(132)

ward, since his death, to confess before men the Saviour whom he served?

His brief military career has left an ineffaceable record upon the officers and the men of his regiment. The testimony of General Doubleday to his competence and fidelity as a staff officer, is given on a preceding page. The following from Major Doubleday, gives additional testimony to his character as an officer of the line:

"On our arrival at Fort Carroll, near Washington, I soon had my attention drawn to his strict and intelligent devotion to his duty, and regard for the health and comfort of the men. At my request he made any suggestions that he thought right, and I invariably found them so.

"We were much together during the whole term of his service. I had often occasion to admire the reliability he showed on all occasions of duty. If he was sent by the General to direct a regiment to a particular position, we always knew that he would do it, though he went without sleep or food.

"A week before his death, I sent him with a party of men up the Leesburg turnpike to get the names of those living near it, and the distances between the houses. This was a kind of work he excelled in, and he went at it with zeal. Towards 4 o'clock, being very warm, he sat down on the ground to make some notes in his field-book, and was remonstrated with by one of the men for doing so, but persisted. The next day, Lieutenant Jones reported to me for duty, in his place, informing me that Gray had taken cold.

"I went down to the bridge in the afternoon, and called from my horse to him, asking how he was. The answer was, he did not feel very well just then—he, like every body else, looking on his illness as a trifling one, a simple cold. Captain Ingalls asked my consent for him to be sent to Georgetown a couple of days after. I supposed he would go to the same place he did in September, and willingly consented. I inquired a day or two after about him, and could learn nothing. I still never dreamed of his being seriously sick, and determined to call on him, when I next went to town. The next news I had was that he was dead.

"I can scarcely realize that I shall never again see him in this world, but I know that he has won admission to a better one. The temptations and debasing vices unhappily so prevalent in camp had no effect on him. No one ever heard impure language or oaths issue from his lips; none knew him to neglect his duty. No soldier need ask for higher praise."

To this testimony to his worth as an officer, may be added the Chaplain's testimony to his character and his services as a Christian:

"There was no officer in our regiment more beloved than Lieutenant Gray; all the officers entertained for him the best of feelings, and the men of his own company thought no one like him. Of these things I am assured. No one in the regiment, perhaps, had a better opportunity than myself to learn these things. So far as my own feelings and affections are concerned, I feel that not only has the regiment been deprived of one of its brightest ornaments and best officers, but that the cause of morality and religion have suffered a great loss in his removal from among us. But 'our loss is his gain.' Lieutenant Gray was always in his place, in the public congregation and the social meeting, active, not only to live out, but to talk out on the great matter of man's best interest.

"As an officer he was strict in discipline, yet always imposed it in such a way as to give his men to understand that it was his duty to give orders, and theirs to obey. His company loved him as a man, and regarded him very much as an officer. He was respected by all the officers of his command, as well as by every soldier."

This testimony of brother officers is fully confirmed by those who were under his command. Sergeant McLean, whose long experience as a seaman before entering the army, had taught him how to discriminate character, states that, at the first, Lieutenant Gray was generally disliked in his company, because of the strictness of his discipline. But he soon overcame the prejudices of the men, and won by degrees their warm and lasting friendship. This the Sergeant ascribes to his military capacity, his personal courage, and his Christian kindness. As illustrative of the Lieutenant's character, McLean states that the regiment was threatened in passing through Baltimore ; Gray, who commanded the rear, ordered three groans to be given in the depot, and then took his place with the men, instead of going into the officer's car, saying, " If there is to be trouble, I want to be near by."

" We were sent out together on one of the worst nights that ever I saw. I have been a sailor for twenty years, and I think I never experienced a worse night than the one I mention. It became my duty to visit and hail the guards, to see that each one was on his post, as it was considered that there was some danger. The night was very dark and very stormy. I came to a certain post, and not being able to discern the guard, I hailed ; when who should answer but Lieutenant Gray. I asked him why he was there, carrying a musket and standing guard. He said the guard on that post was almost perished, and he had sent him to his tent, and was standing his guard. I immediately ordered out another guard to take his place and asked him not to expose himself so much ; ' Well,' he said, ' I am warmly dressed and many of the soldiers are not.' The next time I came around I found him lying on the outside of the tent rolled up in his blanket, and with that exception entirely exposed to the storm ; his excuse then was he did not want to crowd the men, but that night's duty overcame his naturally frail constitution.

" He never shirked his duty as long as he had strength to get out of his tent. At the time I returned from recruiting, there was a fever prevailing which the men thought was contagious. I was called up at midnight to see a sick boy. The Lieutenant heard our conversation, and came out and went with me to see the man. We found him very sick and helpless, and entirely forsaken. The Lieutenant said, ' Stay with him, and I will go and order an ambulance to take him to the hospital. He did so, and he and myself were the only ones to get that sick man out of his tent and into the ambulance, and for fear he would not be well attended to, he went with him ; but the poor fellow's time had come—he died the next day.

" It frequently happened that men were discharged from the hospital and reported for duty, when they were not able to do duty. The only remedy I had was to apply to Lieutenant Gray, and he would get them cleared. Many times it happened that a poor fellow was out of money, and wanted something for his comfort—for our pay-days were, like angels' visits, few and far between —but his hand was always open to charity, and it was closed only in the strong grasp of death."

The nobleness of Gray's character was sometimes strikingly exhibited in little things, where so many betray the meanness they conceal from public view. Upon relinquishing his position on the staff of General Doubleday, he received from a brother officer a handsome offer for his horse. "I should not have allowed you," he answered, "to purchase my horse, for I would not have recommended him. In an action in which we were shelled severely, he acted quite courageously, but afterward, in the battle of Manassas, *he was a coward!* So he would not have suited you."

He who could not brook cowardice in a dumb brute, himself shrank from no danger, but, as one said of him, was ever devoted "to his God, his country, his men and his duty."

The Rev. Alfred Cookman, who was young Gray's pastor at the time when he entered the army, bears testimony to his religious experience in the following affectionate and beautiful tribute :

" REV. J. P. THOMPSON, D. D. :

" MY DEAR BROTHER—I am happy to respond to your wish, and furnish a pastor's brief memorial of the charming virtues and devoted piety of our young friend, Bryant Gray.

" Entering upon the pastorate of the Central or Seventh Avenue M. E. Church in the spring of 1861, I soon formed the acquaintance of this interesting young man. Almost immediately I was impressed with the guilelessness of his spirit, the beautiful modesty of his manners, the noble impulses of his nature, the unusual sprightliness of his mind, and especially his interest and earnestness on the all-important matters of personal piety and Christian usefulness. During the few months we were associated, he was absent from scarcely a single means of grace. In our Sabbath services he was a most attentive hearer, literally drinking in the Word, while in our devotional meetings he was devout and earnest. When he ventured to exercise publicly, either in the form of testimony or vocal prayer, it was always with undisguised timidity, but at the same time with an intelligence, sincerity, and earnestness, that invariably made such exercises interesting and profitable.

"In his connection with the 'Christian Brotherhood' (a most valuable organization of young men in the Central M. E. Church) he was faithful and efficient. No matter what duty was assigned him, he undertook it cheerfully, and executed it energetically and well.

"Our beloved friend was, as your volume will show, not only a more than ordinary young man, but a more than ordinary Christian. Not satisfied with an irregular or spasmodic religious experience, he had strong aspirations for the "Higher Life"—*the life of faith on the Son of God.* Some of our most protracted and edifying conversations were respecting the extent of personal privileges in the gospel. He believed in a full salvation, and was concerned to accept and trust in Christ as a perfect Saviour. I have reason to believe that his consecration was specific and thorough, and that in an exercise of faith he was looking to Christ for that conscious purity which the soul may realize when the blessed Holy Spirit, moment by moment, applies the all-atoning blood to cleanse and keep us clean. This experience will explain the completeness of his Christian character, the vigor of his religious life, and the hallowed nature of his personal influence and usefulness.

" It will involve no violation of confidence or propriety to say, that at that time he was seriously exercised on the subject of the ministry of the Word. A retired parish, a cherished flock, the privilege of cultivating Emmanuel's land and calling sinners to Christ, these were the culmination of his earthly ambition. But in the midst of these day-dreams he heard the tocsin of war! His imperilled nation was calling for help! Himself physically slender and feeble, and so incapacitated for the exposures of a military campaign, his great soul nevertheless promptly responded, and to myself he heroically said, ' I will go ! I have but one life to offer, but oh, how cheerfully will I sacrifice that on the altar of my country's cause !' He went, and, as his subsequent career well shows, God went with him. Oh, what an inspiration for a young man starting out in life, to feel *that the infinite and eternal God is in him, and with him, and for him !* This sentiment is so abundantly illustrated in your memoir of young Gray, that I need not add a word respecting his heroism, fidelity, and usefulness as a Christian soldier.

" I trust that his fellow students of the Free Academy, his large circle of youthful acquaintances, and especially his brother soldiers of our noble army, will be influenced by his beautiful example. Did religion enlarge his views, purify his heart, restrain his life, promote his pleasures, hallow his influence and ennoble his whole nature ?

Did it constitute him a good son, a devoted brother, a conscientious patriot, a brave soldier, a trustworthy friend, and an humble and earnest Christian? Did it make his brief life blessed, and his early death glorious and useful—'for he being dead, yet speaketh?' Did religion do all this for our young friend? Then certainly it is worthy of our immediate and hearty acceptance. Oh, let us conclude and covenant to be like him, 'a good soldier of Jesus Christ,' so that when the battle of life is over, we may hail our departed brother.

> ' Where we shall hear of war no more,
> But ever with our Leader rest,
> On Canaan's peaceful shore.'

Thank God, *the grave of our friend is not the grave of our friendship!*

" Yours, in gospel bonds,

"ALFRED COOKMAN.

" New York, *September* 20, 1864."

13

The poet who crowned his birth with a gift, and his military enlistment with a hymn of consecration, sent this chaplet for our Bryant's tomb :

"New York, *January* 24, 1863.

"My Dear Sir—It was my intention to have written you a letter expressing my sorrow for the death of your son, and I can hardly tell why I have postponed it till now. It seemed but the other day that you informed me of his birth, and now, although he came into the world when I was past the period of middle life, he is in his grave before me. I had taken much interest in watching his progress through life, to its sad but most honorable close. To you, the cup of affliction which has been presented in this dispensation must have been exceedingly bitter. It is sweetened, however, by the reflection that he was prepared for the world upon which he has entered, by a pure, virtuous, and religious life, and that he died in the service of his country. His brief life has not been in vain upon the earth, and having fulfilled, acceptably, we trust, the task assigned him, he goes to his reward, like one called from his labor in the fields to an entertainment in the hall of his employer, before he has endured the ' burden and heat of the day.'

"I am, dear sir, faithfully yours,

" WM. GRAY, Esq.   WM. C. BRYANT."

Another life-long friend of his father, Dr. Thomas Ward, a gentleman well known for his philanthropy and his literary culture, offered his tribute to the memory of the brave young soldier in these worthy lines :

Oh, he was manly, though of age so tender !
    Stern in his duty, gentle in his love :
No foe to truth could bend him to surrender,
    No friend a waver of his faith could prove.

Why should he wither by ignoble fever ?
    Who drank so oft the battle's fiery breath :
Had war no shaft in his remorseless quiver
    To speed his parting with a soldier's death ?

Yet should his name as honored prove in story
    As though he sank beneath contending steel—

Who fell a martyr to his country's glory,
   And shed for her the life-blood of his zeal.

Why in his spring-time must his flower be blasted?
   Bright with the bloom that promised fruit of
      gold:
Unreaped his harvest, and his sowing wasted—
   Stopped in mid-onset—like a steed controlled.

Brave, Christian Knight! still for the right con-
      tending;
   Whose spurs were won even in his youthful
      prime—
Peace, aching heart!—'t is no untimely ending
   Where fruit with flower is borne at blossom-
      time.

THE END.

www.ingramcontent.com/pod-product-compliance
Lightning Source LLC
Chambersburg PA
CBHW021129020726
47500CB00003B/993